My Beloved Waits

Peggy Darty

Heartsong Presents

A note from the author:
I love to hear from my readers! You may correspond with me by writing:

Peggy Darty
Author Relations
PO Box 719
Uhrichsville, OH 44683

ISBN 1-58660-384-1

MY BELOVED WAITS

All Scripture quotations, unless otherwise noted, are taken from the King James Version of the Bible.

Cover illustration by Victoria Lisi and Julius.

PRINTED IN THE U.S.A.

one

Pickens County, Alabama
May 15, 1865

Grace Cunningham shoved the hoe deeper into the potato patch and yanked off her threadbare gloves. "I hate this broken-down hoe!"

"Thou shalt not hate," Elizabeth Cunningham called from the porch.

"And thou shalt not hoe with a splintered handle!" Grace rallied, picking at the splinter in her thumb.

"Thou shalt not hoe isn't any kind of command," Elizabeth called, smiling at her daughter.

Grace pushed the wide-brimmed straw hat back on her blond hair and looked at her mother, who was always reading her Bible.

"Neither is thou shalt not hate," Grace muttered, "but I do."

She couldn't resist getting in the last word, and she felt a whiplash of guilt in her conscience. After losing her father and brother to a senseless war that had destroyed their lives and devastated Riverwood, their little farm, Grace just couldn't have the kind of faith her mother had.

She leaned against the hoe and studied her frail mother.

Mama's pride is damaged too, she thought. The brown hair that had turned gray the past year looked only half-brushed and now slipped carelessly from the chignon, dangling about her face. Grace's father, Fred Cunningham, had promised her that they would always be taken care of, but in spite of his promise, they had ended up broke and alone, struggling to survive.

5

Her father, always conscious of his duties, had worked hard to provide for his family. That sense of duty had compelled him to join Commander Braxton's army in the fall of 1863 when the Union troops were moving deeper into southern territory.

Grace took a deep breath and glanced up at the sky. The noon sun was moving westward, and a gray cloud thickened overhead. The kind of dense heat that usually preceded a thunderstorm was enveloping her like a steam tub. Her scalp itched, and wisps of damp hair bobbed around her cheeks. She yanked off her straw hat and tossed it toward the grass; then she wound the ends of her thick hair around her fingers, skewered it back in a chignon, and adjusted the hairpins.

As she did, her eyes scanned the land bordering the backyard. A dusty, whitewashed cabin had been converted to a storage shed, and the barn, her father's pride, was sadly in need of paint and repair, with buckled boards along the side. Knee-high weeds filled the pasture where a lone mare tossed her head to chase away a horsefly. Mr. Douglas, their neighbor at Oak Grove, had loaned Molly to Grace after the Yanks took their last horse. Molly had a slight limp and could no longer pull a wagon, but Molly and Grace got along just fine. The faithful old mare carried Grace into Whites Creek to trade unused farm tools for garden seeds and food supplies.

Beyond the pasture, paint-chipped fences outlined barren cotton fields stretching to the Tombigbee River. Those fields were the reason her father had brought them from Sand Mountain to Pickens County five years before the war. His dream of growing cotton had come true on the five hundred acres of rich, river-bottom land. In the old days, farmers could get their cotton loaded on boats going downriver to Mobile. But cotton no longer grew along the river's edge.

Grace turned and surveyed her garden. Okra, beans, onions, corn, and potatoes lay beneath the rich soil, holding for her and her mother the promise of better days to come.

"Mother, we're going to have fine Sunday dinners, just like before," she called. "We'll spread the dining table with one of the nice lace tablecloths you treasure, and we'll eat to our heart's content. I can see it now." She swept a hand through the air. "Ripe tomatoes sliced thin on a platter with green onions and sweet pickles. We'll have fried okra, fresh snap beans, creamed corn, and boiled potatoes. Lots of sweet iced tea."

"And fried chicken," her mother offered, her head tilted slightly, her eyes staring dreamily into space.

Grace glanced back at her mother and sighed. She hadn't the heart to remind her there were no chickens to fry and no way to raise their own. Their last six chickens had been taken by Union soldiers. Grace had watched in horror as the soldiers strapped the chickens onto their saddles and rode off with them squawking and flapping. She later learned it was a common practice for soldiers, particularly those in a hurry. At the time, however, she could not believe her eyes as their prize chickens were swept away.

She heaved another sigh, squared her shoulders, and reached for the hoe with new determination. She was finished with the potatoes; time now to thin the corn. Despite the cloud of gloom that hung over the farm she loved so dearly, Grace began to feel a sense of comfort as she thought about the seeds she had planted just a month earlier.

She looked over the neatly weeded rows and remembered how she had waited with anticipation and pride as the seeds began to sprout. Other women could rave about their beautiful flower gardens, but to Grace, true beauty came in vegetables, all colors, sizes, and shapes. She and her mother couldn't eat flowers, but vegetables had half a dozen monetary rewards. She could sell them, cook them, preserve them, swap with her neighbors, or barter with Mr. Primrose at the market in Whites Creek. She could even dry some of her vegetables on cheesecloth over the root cellar and string them on a rope to decorate the kitchen. But that had become a luxury she rarely enjoyed. Nope, these vegetables were for gracing their table and their stomachs, and she smiled at the thought. She picked up the hoe and went back to work.

A few minutes later, Grace heard the whinny of a horse out on the front drive. She glanced at her mother, who was so deep in her reading that she didn't look up as the horse whinnied again. Grace didn't bother to tell her they had company until she went around front to see who was riding the horse. Rarely did anyone come up the drive to their house these days, and that was just fine with Grace.

While she was only nineteen, she had earned the right to be recognized as the boss of Riverwood, and she quickly prepared herself to act in that capacity now. She brushed her hands against the side of her father's overalls to freshen up a handshake, then she hurried around the two-story frame house to the front driveway.

Accustomed to the sight of neighbors, or even the occasional beggar, she came up short as she met the eyes of a stranger riding tall in the saddle on a fine black stallion. For a split second, she was more interested in the horse than its rider, for it was exactly the kind of proud, muscled horse she had always longed to own. The horse had a white blaze on his forehead and three white-stockinged feet.

Her eyes moved from the horse to the man. From the looks of both, it had been a long journey. While the man's dark frock coat and pinstriped trousers were of quality broadcloth, wrinkles in the cloth suggested time in the saddle. He tipped his top hat, revealing dark brown hair that tucked under just above his collar.

She studied his face—long with broad cheekbones and eyes the blue of an October sky. Then he smiled at her, a smile that lit his eyes and showed off a row of even, white teeth. Grace wondered who he was and what he wanted from them.

"Good morning," he said. "My name is Jonathan Parker."

At the sound of his greeting, all admiration of horse and rider fled. Immediately, her spine stiffened. A Yankee!

"What do you want?" she asked bluntly.

He did not flinch at her rude words. Instead his blue eyes, fringed with thick black lashes, looked toward the front porch. "I'd like to speak to Mrs. Cunningham." His tone was polite yet formal.

"She does not receive visitors. My name is Grace Cunningham, and I'm her daughter. What do you want?" she repeated, her gaze slicing up and down his fancy suit and coming again to rest upon his face.

Not a muscle moved in his face in spite of her blunt talk, and she gave him credit for that. Either he was not easily shocked, or he had the ability to conceal his emotions.

She watched him take a long deep breath. She decided he must be reconciling himself to the fact that he would have to deal with her, however unpleasant the task might be.

"I'm on a mission from your father," he said, looking her straight in the eye. "I left him in the military hospital just outside of Chattanooga about three weeks ago. He asked me to return something to his wife."

Grace gasped. "You left Father? In Chattanooga? I thought he was. . .is he. . .?"

She choked on the words, unable to say more. Two years had passed since his last letter; then this February she had seen his name on the list of wounded soldiers in Tennessee. There had been no further word about Fred Cunningham, and he had not returned from the war that had ended just last month. While her mother had never lost faith that he would return, Grace had given up hope.

She blinked, staring into the stranger's face, unable to ask, afraid to hope. Her heart pounded so hard that she pressed her hand to the base of her throat. She could feel the drum of her pulse against her fingertips.

"I'm sorry, but he was dying when I left the hospital, Miss Cunningham."

She swallowed hard, felt her world dip and sway for a moment before she could speak. Then she remembered her manners. "Won't you. . .come up and sit down?" she asked, turning to climb the porch steps and feeling the weakness that had suddenly taken over her legs.

"I'm sorry to be so blunt," he was saying from behind her.

"I left you no choice," she answered, sinking into the cushions on the cane-back rocker. So her father was not coming back home, after all.

She sat there, staring at this stranger, Jonathan Parker, as he swung his long frame down from the saddle and tethered his horse to the rail at the corner of the porch. Then he walked back to his saddlebag and lifted the flap.

She watched his every movement. She had not asked for proof that he had been with her father. His level gaze and sincere manner left no room for doubt. She believed him.

Her eyes widened as he withdrew the black leather Bible she had seen in her father's hands on so many occasions. Then he turned and walked slowly up to the porch. Grace could see the broad muscles of his shoulders straining against his dark frock coat as his climbed the steps and took the chair she had indicated, opposite her.

He was close enough now that she could look him straight in the eye. She realized with a sudden flutter of her heart that he was even more handsome than she had first realized. Her nose twitched at the new scent he trailed over the porch as he passed her. He smelled of fresh pine, as though he had just come from the woods. She liked the smell, and she watched him carefully, taking in everything about him.

"It's been so long since we've had any word from Father. It's just so. . .amazing to think you left him less than a month ago. I have dozens of questions to ask you—"

"Who is it?" Her mother's voice floated from the hallway.

Again, Grace's heartbeat quickened. She looked from the door to Jonathan Parker. "My mother is very fragile now," Grace said under her breath, her eyes imploring this man to understand her meaning. "My only brother was killed at Vicksburg. Then, when it seemed that things could not possibly get worse, our neighbor, Mr. Douglas, saw Father's name on the casualty list at the town hall in Tuscaloosa."

She glanced over her shoulder to the front door to be sure her mother was not on the porch to hear what she was saying. "She. . .has never been the same since we got the heartbreaking news about Father. In some ways, she has lost touch with reality," she finished quickly just as the creak of the door signaled Elizabeth's presence.

Jonathan nodded, turning in his chair to look toward the door where the little woman stood, hesitating to come out.

"Mother, we have a visitor," Grace said. "You will want to hear what he has to say." She looked back at Jonathan. "I think it's time she faced the truth, and I won't shield her from it any longer."

Elizabeth stepped out onto the porch, her head lowered slightly. She glanced quickly at Jonathan Parker.

He stood up, removing his hat. "Hello, Mrs. Cunningham."

Like Grace, the sound of a voice that was not southern startled Elizabeth. She took a step back from him, her hand clutching the door.

"Mother, he brings news about Father."

Elizabeth's eyes widened in shock. It seemed to take a moment for the words to register with her. Then a sob broke from her throat, and she rushed toward Jonathan, reaching for his hand.

"You've seen Fred?" she asked eagerly. Her entire countenance had been transformed by the news. An expression of hope lit her eyes, tilted her mouth upward, and colored her cheeks.

Watching her mother come back to life with false hope, Grace was astonished, and for a moment she felt her heart would break in pieces. Pain racked her emotions, and Grace wanted to scream in agony and rage at the injustice that the war had hurled upon their loving family.

"I left your husband in the military hospital up in Chattanooga," Jonathan Parker said to Elizabeth, speaking in a kind, gentle voice.

Grace went over to stand beside her mother. "Mother, before you get your hopes up," she felt compelled to say, "Mr. Parker has already assured me that Father. . .did not survive."

Her mother shook her head, as though warding off the verbal blow. "No, I won't accept that. Will you please tell me about my Fred?" she asked, still clutching Jonathan Parker's hand as her eyes searched his face.

For a moment, he said nothing. He seemed to be choosing his words as he studied the little woman who clung to him, then he gestured toward the other vacant chair. "Why don't you sit down, Mrs. Cunningham?"

As Jonathan spoke to her mother, Grace smiled sadly. She was touched by his sensitive nature. She wanted to tell him how grateful she was for the way he so tactfully delivered the heartbreaking news.

"Allow me to explain, Mrs. Cunningham," he said, as they took their seats. "Your husband saved my life. I was a soldier in the Union army. I had been captured in north Georgia by a Confederate officer. We were on our way back to his camp on the Tennessee line. Late that evening, while he was asleep, I managed to break free of the ropes. I took his uniform." He paused, glancing at Grace. "But I did not harm him. He had fed me and treated me decently. I tied him up and took his horse, but I knew his men would find him the next morning."

He paused, turning his eyes toward the overgrown front lawn. "That night I had to work my way through a dense briar thicket, and I ended up with scratches on my hands and face." A grim little smile touched his lips as he glanced back at Grace. "I looked as though I'd been in battle. My right hand was bleeding, so I cleaned my hand with a handkerchief, then tied the handkerchief about my throat. The blood-stained handkerchief appeared to serve as a bandage, supporting my hand gestures to indicate a throat injury. I knew if I were to escape enemy territory. . ." He broke off, glancing from Grace to her mother, as though regretting his choice of words.

"Go on," Grace prompted, scooting to the edge of the seat as she waited to hear the rest of the story.

"It was convenient for me to point to my throat and pretend to be unable to speak. Under this guise, I rode into a Confederate camp on the outskirts of Chattanooga. Your father was the first person who befriended me. That night we were attacked by another battalion of Union soldiers, and before I could explain who I was, I was beaten senseless." He paused and dropped his head, silent for a moment. Then he looked back at Grace. "When I regained consciousness I realized I was imprisoned with the Confederates in a Federal camp in Chattanooga. I was in the cell with your father, and he was very kind to me. In fact, he was willing to share his last piece of bread with me. I'll never forget that," he said quietly.

"That's the way Fred is," Elizabeth said, smiling through her tears. "He always considers the needs of others."

Jonathan hesitated and glanced across at Grace. She knew he had caught the use of the present tense when her mother spoke of the man she loved with all of her heart.

"I had identification papers in my boot," Jonathan continued. "When finally I convinced the guards who I was, they provided me with a horse and allowed me to take your father to a military hospital. By this time, of course, he knew the truth about me, but it no longer mattered."

"I'm sure he was just so grateful that you saved him," Grace said, fighting to hold back her tears.

Beneath her tomboy-tough exterior, she was almost as sensitive as her mother. But she was younger and hardier, and she knew she had to be strong for both of them. Yet as she sat listening to the story, the image Jonathan portrayed to them of her dear father, starving in a prison camp, had almost broken her heart.

"We had no idea what he had been through," Grace said, feeling the quiver of her lower lip. She caught her lip between her teeth and looked quickly at her mother. She had tried for the past two years to shield her mother from more heartache. Yet this man seemed to understand exactly how much he could say and the manner in which to say it. For her mother had not dissolved in tears or cried out at the cruel fate of her husband.

Grace looked from her mother's sweet face to the tall, dark-haired man who sat beside her, turning the rim of his hat around and around in his hands as he told the story. In the last hour, he had ridden up their drive and turned their entire world upside down. She had lost all sense of time and place; she was vaguely aware of the mourning dove in the oak overhead. Its plaintiff little cry seemed a fitting accompaniment to the words Jonathan Parker spoke.

"I appreciate your coming here, Mr. Parker." Elizabeth's voice filled the momentary silence. "I have prayed so many times for my husband's safety," she said, turning in her seat, casting her gaze toward the front drive that wound beneath the canopy of oaks and disappeared around the curve.

"I count it a privilege to be able to visit you, Mrs. Cunningham. I promised your husband that I would return and tell you what had happened to him. Oh, and I have something to give you." He reached for the worn Bible that had been placed on the low wooden table beside his chair.

As her eyes followed his gesture, Grace realized that she had been so caught up in the story that she had completely forgotten he was returning her father's Bible. Now all eyes were on the book that Jonathan held carefully in his hand.

Elizabeth gave a small cry. "It is my Fred's Bible," she said, staring at the chipped leather.

"Yes, it is," Jonathan said, extending it to her. "Your husband gave it to me and asked that I bring it to you, that I put it in your hands. I believe those were the words he used."

Elizabeth stood up and walked over to accept the Bible.

"I tried to be very careful with it," Jonathan said, and as he spoke his brows drew together in a frown, as though he might have accidentally damaged the precious Bible on the long trip to Riverwood.

Elizabeth examined the Bible from front to back, then briefly flipped through the pages.

"Oh, yes, it's in good condition. Thank you so very much," she said, hugging the Bible to her breast as one would welcome a lost child.

"I'm sure this Bible was a great comfort to my husband," Elizabeth said, looking back at Jonathan.

"Yes, it seemed to be. Many men kept Bibles with them during the war. In fact, I heard of one incident where a soldier was carrying a Bible under his shirt, and it stopped a bullet." He looked down, as though he had said too much.

"Thank you for bringing this to me," Elizabeth said softly, then she turned and opened the front door and went back inside the house. Her steps echoed down the hallway, and Grace could hear her climbing the stairs to her bedroom.

Grace took a deep breath and looked at Jonathan. "It's been very difficult for her to accept the truth that Father isn't coming home. She still sits out here every afternoon, watching the driveway, expecting him to return. I've tried to convince her otherwise."

"I'm so sorry," he said. The blue eyes seemed to deepen as he spoke to her. He tilted his head to the side and looked at her.

She shook her head and blinked, trying again to absorb everything he had told them. As the silence stretched, she felt such gratitude to him for being so kind to her father that she knew what her father would expect in return.

"Please, come inside and allow me to prepare a meal for you." She glanced at the black stallion, nipping at the thick grass on the neglected lawn. She was glad that it was benefitting this man's horse. "What about water for your horse? And feed?" she asked.

"Both would be welcome. Please don't go to any trouble. I don't want to impose on you."

"You're not. This is the least we can do for you. We owe you a debt of gratitude," she said, looking at his handsome face and trying not to feel overwhelmed by a man so kind and caring, yet so handsome and appealing.

As though he felt he needed to break the spell, he stood and looked around. "Shall I take General—er, my horse— around back?"

She remembered the watering trough and the feed bucket. "Yes, the barn is in poor condition, but you are welcome to it. We lost all of our cattle and horses, although we never had a lot. Father was a small landowner compared to the others in the area. He came to this area from North Alabama with his parents, who were migrant workers. He worked hard and saved his money; eventually he was able to buy land here. With each successful cotton harvest, he bought a few more acres, or he and Mother did some work on the house."

Grace thought back over the years. Her father had always

wanted the best for his family and had done everything he could to be sure that she and Freddy went to church, attended school, and grew into responsible people.

"As you know, my father was a very good man," she said, remembering the long hard hours her father had toiled. She stood up, thinking of her promise. "Make yourself at home while I prepare lunch."

As she opened the front door and stepped inside the hall, she could see Jonathan speaking affectionately to his horse. He seemed to be a kind man, and she liked him very much. She was so grateful that her father had miraculously met a man like Jonathan Parker to take care of him and fulfill his deathbed wish. She swallowed hard and hurried on down the hall.

When she entered the kitchen, she was suddenly aware of how empty and lonely the large room seemed to her. This room had for many years been filled with people, and it was a joyous place. The echo of laughter from this room had seemed to flow through the entire house. Her mother loved entertaining neighbors and friends, and she had done it often and with exceeding grace and kindness.

Grace's gaze wandered to the trestle table, pushed into the far corner. If a large group of children were not invited as well, she and Freddy often dined in the kitchen while their parents entertained guests. Most of the time, however, entire families came and stayed for several days. Those had been wonderful days and months and years, and all of it seemed to Grace like a wonderful and special dream to cherish for the rest of her life.

She took a deep breath and closed her eyes. All of that was gone now, and even though she was happy to have met Jonathan Parker, he had just confirmed one more sad and devastating truth: her father was never coming back to Riverwood.

"I just can't think about it," she said. And she couldn't. For a moment she wondered if at times she was running from reality as much as her mother was. She shook her head and forced her thoughts to the business of preparing lunch. Turning, she headed toward the pantry.

The pantry was a small room that reeked of green onions and pepper and spices from the floor to the ceiling. The long side walls held deep sturdy shelves which in years past had held an entire winter's supply of preserved vegetables and fruits and baskets of potatoes. The end wall had hooks and nails from top to bottom for hanging baskets and buckets of kitchen items.

But these days, the room that had held such an abundance of food looked empty and forlorn. At least they still had jars of dried beans and preserved apples and a basket with new potatoes and some green onions from the garden. Grace cheered herself with the vision of all the vegetables in her garden lining the shelves after the harvest. This winter she and her mother would have better food. She would see to that. There would be snap beans to string, potatoes to peel, and tender young corn that could be prepared half a dozen ways.

For now she would make do with what she had. And she would grease a skillet and bake up a batch of her crusty corn bread. She smiled to herself. Mr. Jonathan Parker would not leave Riverwood with an empty stomach.

two

When Grace, her mother, and Jonathan were seated at the dining table, Grace watched with satisfaction as Jonathan ate heartily and exercised the table manners she had been taught to appreciate.

"This is a wonderful meal," he said, looking across the table at her.

"Thank you." Grace shifted in her chair, suddenly aware of how stiff the overalls felt against her skin. She imagined she must look quite unladylike to this man, who had obviously been well reared and was probably accustomed to dining with ladies in fine gowns.

"I enjoy cooking," she said, trying to forget her silly idea of ladies in gowns. "I'm just grateful Ardella left behind her recipes. She was the best cook in all of the world," she added, her eyes clouding over as she spoke of Ardella. "Ardella and William lived here with us all of their lives, but they were never slaves," she added quickly. "Father paid them well and told them they were free to go whenever they wanted." She shook her head. "Fortunately for us, they never wanted to leave."

"I can hear the affection in your voice when you mention their names," Jonathan said.

Elizabeth pressed her lace handkerchief to her eyes and dropped her head. Jonathan was quick to notice, and he quickly lifted his cup and began to inspect it. "This is a beautiful cup," he said. "It looks as though it may have been handcrafted in England."

"Fred ordered the set for my fortieth birthday," Elizabeth

announced, looking up with shining eyes.

"He was a very thoughtful man," Jonathan acknowledged.

Grace cleared her throat. "Where is your home, Mr. Parker?"

"Please call me Jonathan," he said and smiled at her. Then he looked back at her mother, as though reminding himself to include her in the conversation as well. "I was born and raised in Kentucky. Our farm was 480 acres on the edge of Louisville. We used three small fields to grow all the vegetables to eat; one large field was for growing corn for our feed for hogs, chickens, cattle, and of course for corn meal. The farm was primarily used for raising cattle. My father furnished beef for the riverboats up and down the Ohio and for passenger trains traveling through Louisville."

"That sounds like a good life," Elizabeth said thoughtfully.

Jonathan nodded. "It was until '60 when my father came down with a lung disease and required a lot of medical care. To pay medical expenses, I sold most of the cattle we owned. He died a month before the war broke out. . . ." His voice trailed for a moment, and Grace watched him closely as she listened. She wanted to know everything about him, and she was very curious about the family he had mentioned.

"Do you have brothers and sisters?" she asked.

"I have two sisters. An older sister, Louise, is married to a furniture merchant in Louisville. They have five children. Katherine, my younger sister, was only twelve when I left for war. In my last letter from Mother, she wrote that she and Katherine had moved to Louisville to live with Louise and her husband."

As always, Grace was thinking of the land. "Who's taking care of your farm for you?"

He frowned. "I don't know, and I must admit I'm quite concerned about it. I wrote my brother-in-law, asking him to hire someone to go out and take care of things, but I haven't heard back from him in months."

Grace watched his frown deepen, and she could imagine he must be very worried about his home. "I expect you need to get back to Kentucky," she said.

"Thank you so much for making this long trip to bring us news," Elizabeth added, looking at him with sincere appreciation.

"Yes, we appreciate you keeping your promise to Father."

He smiled at her, that sad, gentle smile that was beginning to tear at Grace's heart. "As I told you, your father saved my life. Making this trip was not much to do in return. I'm only sorry I couldn't bring you good news."

Grace glanced at her mother and saw her drop her gaze. Hoping to change the subject, Grace asked, "So what plans do you have for your farm when you return?"

"I'm hoping to restock the cattle," he said. "And in time I'd like to raise horses. Kentucky is thoroughbred country, and its always been my dream to have fine horses."

Grace stared at him. *It's been my dream too*, she thought. But of course she would never admit that to him. Still, it was nice to think that someone might be able to make such a dream come true.

Jonathan looked from Grace to her mother. "Everyone must put the past behind them and go on, although I'm certain that is a very difficult thing for you to do."

"Yes, but you're right," Grace joined in. "We can't go on living in the past." She glanced at her mother, hoping she would take those words to heart.

Elizabeth smiled as she reached for the small jar of pear preserves they had put up last fall.

"Every woman in the South is taught to preserve the fruit on our many trees, Jonathan. Grace, how many fruit trees are left?"

"We had a bad storm last fall that damaged some of our trees," Grace explained. "Two of our apple trees still bear fruit, and of course the pear tree down in the corner of the yard."

"And you were able to preserve the fruit?" Jonathan inquired.

Grace smiled easily at that. "Oh yes. Apple butter, apple-sauce, dried apple pies, and pear preserves. Lots of pear preserves."

"Every southern girl carries the special family recipes in her hope chest," her mother said, looking at Grace with obvious affection.

"And do you have a hope chest?"

No, because I have no hope, she thought, giving their guest a penetrating stare.

Jonathan had laid down the linen napkin and was looking at Grace with those blue, blue eyes that had begun to make her a little bit nervous, particularly when they seemed to take in every feature on her face. She wondered what he thought about her sunburned nose and her plain face, void of pressed powder or rouge or any of the items fancy ladies wore. Then she remembered his question and delighted in her independence. It was her one claim to being her own person.

"No, I don't. I'm afraid I defied tradition when it comes to keeping a hope chest," she said, aware of the edge to her tone. She gave a light shrug, and the pale blue work shirt beneath her overalls scratched at her right shoulder blade. "It always seemed a bit silly to me. No offense, Mother," she added quickly.

"You never wanted a hope chest," Elizabeth said, looking rather sad.

"Miss Grace," Jonathan said, startling her with the formality of his address, "do you have friends living nearby?"

Grace hesitated. She had preferred the company of Freddy's friends, even though they were five years older, to the giddy-headed girls in the community who were closer to her own age.

"We were quite young when the war broke out," she answered, looking him squarely in the eye. "Some of the girls accepted proposals from neighborhood boys heading off to war. It was their way of aiding the cause."

She watched Jonathan's head tilt slightly, and she knew he was following her line of sarcasm, while her mother merely smiled, looking pleased at the idea of aiding the cause.

"Sue Ann, my closest friend, moved to Mobile to live with her grandmother, and Rose Marie, our closest neighbor, married Charles Raymond Anderson, whose farm adjoined theirs near Whites Creek. It was a nice way to unite families and land, particularly the land," she added, smiling sweetly as her gaze traveled from Jonathan to her mother, who smiled back.

When she met Jonathan's eyes, however, she saw the slight quirk of his lips, and she sensed that she hadn't fooled him for one minute. This man was smart, very smart, Grace told herself. Her veiled sarcasm would not be lost on him. She even suspected that he was very good at reading minds, and at that, she began to fiddle with her silverware.

Distant thunder rumbled over the roof of the house. Elizabeth began fidgeting in the mahogany chair. "I think it's going to rain," she said, looking disturbed. "And now we can't sit out on the front porch this evening." She turned back to Jonathan. "Every day I sit there, watching and waiting for Fred. He promised me he would return from the war."

Grace stared at her mother. Was she going to pretend that Jonathan had not told them her father was dying when he last saw him? She glanced across at Jonathan and saw that he was looking toward the window. She guessed he was trying to avoid the subject.

Grace opened her mouth, then closed it again. This was no time to remind her mother of the cruel truth, she decided. Instead, she followed Jonathan's gaze to the window where the mimosa bush had begun to tremble as the breeze picked up into a steady wind.

"Mother is right," Grace said. "You shouldn't be out on a stormy night. It will get dark early, and there are deep ruts in the road when it rains. Sometimes thieves lurk in the woods along the roads."

"And you two ladies live here alone?" he asked, looking from one to the other with a deep frown rumpling his smooth brow.

"The neighbors are very kind to look in on us," Grace explained, "although we manage just fine."

He studied her face for a moment, as though weighing her words. "I imagine that you do," he said with a smile.

Grace was grateful that he didn't respond to the sharp tone in her voice; when her independence was questioned, she had learned to rally back.

"I will accept your kind offer on the condition that you allow me to do something for you in the morning before I leave."

"Like what?" Grace inquired.

"Forgive me for saying so, but I noticed as I turned up the driveway this afternoon that the gate is broken. Your reference to thieves in the woods concerns me. I'll stay if you allow me to repair the gate. It shouldn't take long, and I promise not to overstay my welcome."

"It's settled then," Elizabeth said, looking extremely pleased—a look Grace rarely saw on her mother's face.

Another explosion of thunder shook the teacups in their saucers. Grace glanced through the lace curtains to the side lawn, where an eerie yellow light tinged the afternoon. Pale white light flickered and zigzagged past the window.

The mimosa bushes quivered, and overhead the thick branches of trees heaved as debris flew about.

"It's getting worse," Grace said, glancing at Jonathan, who had walked over to stand beside her. She was surprised to see that his face had turned pale, and his eyes had widened as he stared out the window. He looked as though he were becoming ill.

"What is it?" she asked.

He turned to face her. The muscles in his face clenched, and his blue eyes held a terrible kind of fear.

"What's wrong?" she touched his sleeve.

He shook his head and passed a hand over his eyes. "Just a bad memory. Forgive me."

"Of course," she said, wondering why the storm affected him so.

Then the very foundation of the house seemed to quiver as thunder blasted again and again. Something crashed in the front of the house, and Grace rushed out of the dining room and down the hall to see what was happening.

In the parlor, she felt the rush of the wind. A corner of the drape flew about the east window, and as she hurried in that direction, she saw shards of glass strewn about the floor. The empty tea pitcher she had left out on the window ledge had been blown back against the window, shattering a small corner of it. Now remnants of the glass pitcher and the window were being tossed about like dust bunnies.

Seizing a small pillow from the sofa, she stepped around the edge of the glass and quickly stuffed the thick pillow into the gaping hole. Immediately, the wind softened.

"What is it? What's happened?" Jonathan asked from the doorway.

She turned to see that he looked more pale than before, and she began to feel alarmed for him. He was obviously fighting some illness.

"I'm afraid I carelessly left a tea pitcher out on the window ledge when I was pruning the shrubs yesterday," she explained. "The wind blew it against the window and broke a piece of glass. It's okay," she said, trying to keep her voice calm and soothing. "Why don't you sit down? You don't look well at all."

He sank into the chair and again passed his hand over his forehead. Grace noticed the frayed threads along the sides of the chair and the chip in the mahogany arm. The furnishings were in sad condition, but there was nothing she could do about it, and Jonathan seemed not to notice.

"I must apologize," he began.

"Perhaps I am the one who should apologize. I fear my food has poisoned you."

"No, it's not the food."

"I'll get you some water."

She hurried back to the dining room, where her mother was getting up from the chair. "Is everything all right?" she asked calmly. Despite the fierce storm taking place outside, her mother did not look troubled.

"Yes. Mother, why don't you go up and lie down? You always say you sleep best when it is raining."

"Oh, I do. Will Mr. Parker be staying overnight?"

She nodded. "Yes, I think so. The storm is too bad to allow him to leave now."

Grace hurried into the kitchen to pour a tumbler of water from a pitcher. What was wrong with him? she wondered. Had he been injured in the war?

As she passed through the hall, she saw her mother climbing the stairs. At least her mother was not aware of the man's sudden illness. It would be like her mother to try and put him to bed and insist he stay on for a week.

When Grace returned to the parlor, Jonathan was standing before the broken window, surveying the damage.

"Here's some water for you," she said, as he turned and crossed the room to her side.

"You seem to have temporarily repaired the damage," he said, indicating the pillow. He accepted the glass of water, drank it, and handed the glass back to her. "I'm afraid the war is still with me," he said, glancing back at the gray day beyond the window. "Whenever I hear heavy thunder, for a moment I'm back in battle."

She sat down on the settee and looked at him. "Would it help to talk about it?"

He sat down in the chair again, cradling his head in his hands. "It's the same memory every time. We're camped for the night after a thirty-six hour ride. Men were falling asleep in the saddle, and we had to stop and bed down for the night in a wooded area. We were awakened from a dead sleep by the sound of cannon fire at daybreak. When I looked around, we were surrounded by Confederate infantry; it didn't seem we had a chance. We tried to move deeper into the woods while soldiers were coming at us with clubbed carbines and sabers. We had masked our guns in pine thickets the night before, and we opened fire. The wounded began to fall. . . gray coats, blue coats, soldiers piling up together. . ." His voice was softly muffled by his fingers covering his face.

The keening wind and biting rain hit the window as he spoke, but he didn't seem to notice. Even Grace scarcely heard it as she stared at the man relating a memory that was obviously horrible to recall. He had stopped talking, and she took a deep breath.

"How did you manage to escape?" she asked gently.

"I'm not sure. I just remember firing and backing up, further and further into the woods. Then I heard a bugle, and I barely made out a column of our cavalry riding into the battle. Somehow they turned the Rebs back just in time. I stumbled down a bank to a creek and fell in. Then. . .when I looked around, I saw the water was red. . .and I saw some of my men lying there. . .their heads in the water. . . ."

He stopped talking, and Grace said nothing. He had painted the scene quite vividly for her, and she felt sick just thinking about it. When he spoke of Federal and Confederate soldiers dying together, it was almost too appalling to imagine; yet in her mind's eye she had seen it all. She wondered how he could possibly have survived.

"I am so sorry," he said, removing his hands from his face and looking at her with sad, bleak eyes. "I have no right to tell you such a horrible story. I have forgotten my place," he said, coming to his feet. "I will leave now."

"No, that isn't necessary," she said. "It is late, and Mother wants you to stay."

Grace realized as she spoke the words that she was using her mother's wish to justify her decision, but it didn't matter. He had told her something quite personal—she knew that—and in doing so, had somehow bridged the awkward gap between them.

She looked across at the broken window and saw that the pillow had worked wonders in keeping out the wind and rain. The rain had stopped, but the storm laid a bleak gray light over the land. Grace got up and lit the lamps. She smiled as she realized that for once, she would not awake in the night, jumping at a strange sound, worrying that a thief might be breaking in. She would feel protected with Jonathan Parker staying in the guest room.

She was borrowing misery if she took comfort from the thought of having a man under their roof. He would be leaving tomorrow, and she would never see him again. That realization felt as heavy in her mind as the thick humidity settling over the room after the rain.

"Will your mother be joining us?" he asked.

"No, probably not for awhile. She tires easily and usually goes to bed rather early. But then, she is so glad to have you visiting that she may surprise me and come downstairs for more conversation."

"I hope she does."

He cleared his throat, and his voice was stronger when he spoke. "I know the news I have brought about your father is painful."

"Yes. But it feels good to be able to talk with someone who

was with Father at. . .at the end." She leaned forward. "Tell me more about him."

Jonathan was quiet for a moment as his eyes lifted over her head to something outside the window. "He spoke of you and your mother constantly. I soon came to realize that he was an amazing man."

She swallowed hard. "What was wrong with him? Other than starvation, I mean."

"He had dysentery. It was rampant among the soldiers, and conditions in the hospital left something to be desired. But it was the fever that had begun to take his life. I would not have left him alone at the end, but the nurse convinced me that the outbreak of fever was contagious. I had to think about returning to Kentucky."

"Of course," Grace said, wondering if her father had suffered very much. But she couldn't bring herself to ask anything more. The pain was too great. Then she thought of one more thing, still holding onto one last hope. "Was he. . .conscious when you left?"

Jonathan looked at her with compassion. "No, he was not."

Silence filled the room until he sighed. "After he gave me the Bible, he seemed to fade away. I'm. . .so sorry."

The bitterness that had festered in her heart like an ugly sore suddenly burst open. Grace jumped up from the love seat, hugging her arms around herself.

"It's all so unfair!" she cried, pacing around the room. "I don't know how Mother keeps her faith or why she bothers. Good people die; horrible people kill and go free. Nothing makes sense to me."

"I know. I was always amazed at your father's faith. My parents were not as devout, and I learned quite a bit from him in the short time we were together."

The words he spoke fell into the tense silence, and for the first time all evening, Grace was conscious again of the difference in his voice and her own. She thought about the difference between his background and hers and the fact that he had fought opposite her father and brother. Yet, she had sat and listened to his horrid account of fighting between her side and his, and for a moment, both sides had seemed to blend into one terrible tragedy. But they were separate tragedies, and the South had suffered defeat.

"You look troubled," he said, watching her closely.

She blinked and looked away. "Tired," she replied. "I'm tired. If you'll excuse me, I think I'll go on up to my room. It's been a long day."

"Yes, of course."

"Mother has prepared the guest room for you. The third door on the right upstairs." She glanced toward the darkness beyond the window, then back at him. "Well, good night."

Turning, she hurried down the hall and up the stairs to her room, desperately needing her privacy. She was grateful her mother had faithfully lit the upstairs candelabra, for its soft glow offset the gloom. Yet it did not reach the shadowed corners of the long upper hall, which greeted her every evening.

With each step, Grace's feet felt heavier. Her heart seemed to be dropping to her feet as she lit the lamp on the table beside the door in her bedroom. Then slowly she turned and closed the door.

Exhaustion crept over her as she walked to the armoire and pulled out her nightclothes. She was tired of dealing with the conflicting emotions that were a part of her every waking moment. War, death, poverty, loneliness. And now she had spent several hours with an interesting man, a *Northerner,* who was sure to set the tongues wagging throughout the county.

That didn't bother her. What bothered her was the fact that she had been cheated once again. Fate had dangled an enticing dream before her, then just as quickly, and as cruelly, yanked it away. She had no hope of having a husband and a family. The future that stretched before her was bleak and unexciting.

As she tied the strings on the bodice of her nightgown, she began to wish she hadn't asked Jonathan Parker to stay overnight. It would have been so much easier to thank him for his trouble, then send him on his way.

She walked to her bedroom window and stared out at the dark night. The wind sighed through the branches, a low moan that seemed to echo the mood in her heart. Despite the humidity of the May evening, a chill crept over her skin as she turned from the window and walked across the room to extinguish the light.

She would be relieved when Jonathan Parker climbed on his black stallion and rode out of their lives, she thought as she crawled into her feather bed and settled into the softness. She closed her eyes, but in the next second, deep blue eyes looked into her own, and the handsome face of the stranger under their roof lingered in her memory.

She rolled over and flopped against the pillow, angry again. She didn't need to be reminded of what she was missing for the rest of her life.

three

When Grace stirred against her pillow the next morning, she knew before she opened her eyes that something had changed in her life. Something was different about today. What was it? She stretched her slim body against the linen sheet as her memory settled in place. Suddenly, she bolted upright. *Jonathan Parker!*

Tossing back the covers, she hurried to the washstand, lifted the china pitcher, and poured water into the bowl. The morning ritual of splashing water on her face to wake up was unnecessary today. She was wide awake as she began to bathe, using the special lilac soap she hoarded.

Her eyes fell on the sweat-stained overalls, crumpled in a heap in the corner of the bedroom. Sniffing, she tweaked her nose in disgust. Mr. Jonathan Parker wouldn't be seeing her in overalls today. No, sir! Her mind moved on to the possibilities of her wardrobe, though they were slim.

When she finished her bath, she stepped over the overalls and hurried to the armoire, determined to feel the softness of a dress against her skin. She had not worn crinolines in a very long time, one of the advantages of their distressed situation, but today she intended to enjoy every minute she had with their charming Kentucky guest. Today she would enjoy being a woman. She felt surprisingly good about their northern house visitor in the bright sunlight of a new spring day. The morbid thoughts of the night before had been washed away by a deep sleep, just as the hard rain had polished the leaves of the magnolia tree to a waxy green and scrubbed up the sky to a fresh clean blue. She was ready to be up and about her business, to face life again.

Reaching inside the armoire, she withdrew a pair of lacy pantaloons. Turning to the wardrobe, she chose the dress with tiny pink rosebuds that always made her think of flower gardens in the spring. While she dressed, she studied her reflection in the mirror.

She had been blessed with clear skin. While her nose always managed to hang onto the first sunburn, the rest of her skin turned a light golden tan once she adjusted to the sun. Wide-set hazel eyes beneath sharply arched brows stared back at her as she lifted a work-roughened hand to the deep hollow in her cheek. She had lost more weight, and dark circles showed beneath her lashes. Another year of drudgery and she would be skin and bones, she thought, frowning suddenly. She reached up and smoothed the little wrinkle from her brow. There was no point in thinking about life's unpleasantness now; she wanted this to be a good day.

She reached for the silver-handled hair brush and worked it through her tangled blond hair as she thought about the day ahead. Why not relish gazing at the handsome man, talking to him, maybe even flirting a little bit? After all, he would soon be only a memory, so she should make it a good one.

She whisked her hair back from her face and secured it with a black grosgrain ribbon at the nape of her neck. Then her fingers darted up to fan the wavy ends out across her shoulders. The vinegar rinses she put on her hair kept the shine in it, which always surprised her, considering how little time she had to take care of herself.

Placing her hands on each side of her narrow waist, she whirled before the mirror, satisfied that she achieved her goal: she looked and felt like a woman.

She hurried out of the room and down the steps, led by the sound of voices from somewhere below. At the bottom step, she turned her head toward the open front door. Following the voices, she sauntered up the hall to peer out on the front porch. Beyond the round white columns that rose to the roof, Grace could see rain drops, like crystal beads, glimmering on the thick grass in the yard. While the yard was pitifully overgrown, like all of the land, a timeless beauty lingered in the massive oaks with their brawny arms and in the creamy blossoms on the magnolia tree.

"Weeping may endure for a night, but joy cometh in the morning. . . ."

Grace winced. Her mother was quoting Scripture again, probably boring their guest to death.

"You are a very inspiring lady," Jonathan was saying.

Grace quirked an eyebrow. He didn't sound bored; there was even a pleasant note in his voice.

Curiosity tingled through her, as titillating as the fresh breeze from a light east wind. She opened the door and stepped out onto the porch.

"Hello, Dear."

Grace turned to study her mother. Her hazel eyes were glowing, and a smile slipped easily over her lips. The look of happiness on her mother's face warmed Grace's heart.

"Good morning," she said, glancing at her father's Bible, which lay open in her mother's lap. She imagined her mother probably sat up half the night, reading the Bible her father had sent back with Jonathan.

"Good morning." Jonathan rose to his feet as she approached.

"Good morning," she said, meeting Jonathan's friendly smile.

He had changed into a fresh white shirt, and his hair was neatly combed. He seemed taller, even more masculine, she thought, as she passed by him on her way to the rocker.

"Jonathan is a Christian, Grace. He was telling me how, as a boy, he sat at his mother's feet while she read Scripture."

Grace looked from her delighted mother to Jonathan. A nagging suspicion rose in Grace's mind as her eyes lingered on Jonathan. He was not at all embarrassed by her mother's reference to him being a Christian. Grace knew that Freddy would never want anyone going on about that, even though he had been baptized in Caney Creek years ago at the age of eleven.

She tilted her head and looked at Jonathan more closely, trying to figure him out. He merely smiled and turned back to her mother, who was absolutely doting on him.

Elizabeth was as excited as a little girl at a tea party. "I favor the Psalms," she was saying. "Grace, do you remember how your father and I loved to read those passages?" She glanced at Grace.

"Oh yes," Grace replied, still watching Jonathan, although she had not managed to make him uncomfortable. Since he didn't seem perturbed by her staring, she decided to take a good long look in the bright sunlight of morning.

He had broad cheeks with prominent cheekbones and a smooth straight nose. She had a fleeting desire, a rather crazy one, to show him off to Rose Ann, who had spent most of her teenage years doting on the male population. Then as Jonathan made a comment to her mother, she heard his voice and realized that Rose Ann would have something ugly to say about his being a Yankee. She sighed and turned her attention back to her mother.

Elizabeth was looking out across the lawn, and for a moment it seemed that she was watching something that no one else could see.

"Grace, do you recall how you and Freddy would play on that swing for hours at a time?"

Grace followed her mother's eyes to the huge oak in the corner of the yard. From the lowest branch, the rope swing hung, lonely and unused through the years. She blinked, as the vision of a little girl giggling while her older brother pushed the swing filled her mind.

"Yes, I do," she answered, feeling the first threat of sadness. The day had started so perfectly. Why did her mother have to go and ruin it? But then she was merely recalling a fond memory, and that should not ruin a day. But a happy memory merely emphasized how unhappy so much of her life had become.

Jonathan cleared his throat. "How old was Freddy when he joined the army?"

Grace dragged her memory back through the years. She looked at Jonathan, and a sad little smile touched her lips as she recalled her headstrong brother. "Freddy had just turned seventeen when he and the neighbor boys got all worked up about being soldiers. Father pleaded with him to wait another year. There were crops in the field and dozens of chores left undone. But Freddy was strong willed."

"Our little boy turned into a soldier overnight," Elizabeth mused, still staring at the swing.

Grace nodded. "He couldn't wait to tell us good-bye and meet up with the Walkers and the three Estes brothers. They were all so eager to gallop off to war." Her voice was mocking as she spoke. She felt the bitterness welling up inside her.

She looked back at Jonathan. "Like Freddy, the Estes brothers never returned."

"Are you going to make coffee?" Elizabeth asked suddenly.

When Grace looked at her, it seemed her mother had not heard the sad words she had just spoken. Sometimes she longed to be like her mother for a short while, to blot out all the bad memories and cling to the good. She supposed it made it easier to hang on to her faith.

It was not until he stood that she realized she had made Jonathan feel uncomfortable. "I'll get busy on the gate."

"And I'll make coffee," she said, thinking that they would

all go on about their business now. Yet it was a relief to have something simple to do, anything to occupy her mind and her hands. She headed toward the door, glancing again at her mother, who was staring out across the lawn, deep in thought. She did not appear troubled or even unhappy. She was simply lost in her own world.

Grace hurried toward the kitchen. Strong coffee was exactly what she needed to jolt some sense back into her befuddled brain. Maybe Jonathan Parker was the most handsome man she had ever seen and maybe even the nicest, if she didn't count her father. But he was a Yankee, she reminded herself as she poured water from the teakettle into the iron pot and placed it over the low fire in the hearth. Despite her silly notion about flirting with him and having something to remember later, she realized that she had to be practical. She couldn't lounge about the porch daydreaming like her mother. Someone here had better face reality.

From the pantry, she removed the small tin canister of coffee, so precious during the war that she and her mother rationed themselves miserably. She had derived great satisfaction from bartering an old saddle from the stable in exchange for some much-needed staples. When she'd accompanied her closest neighbors, the Douglas family, to Tuscaloosa, she had enjoyed herself tremendously. Like her father, she loved to trade, and now she made a mental note to gather up anything she could find in the barn and outbuildings. She would plan another day of trading, and that thought helped to lift her spirits.

She walked back to the pot and poured out a small portion of the freshly ground coffee. Maybe she'd check with Agnes Douglas to see when they would be returning to town. It would be something to look forward to after Jonathan left.

The heavy tread of boots in the hall reminded her that the man in question had not left and was, in fact, headed toward the kitchen.

"Where might I find some tools?" he asked politely.

She walked to the kitchen window and pointed out the small building huddled near the barn. "The few tools we have left will be there. To be honest, I haven't even been in to look around lately. For awhile, I checked every day to be sure no one was hiding there."

He stared at her in dismay. "Do you have a gun, Grace?"

She smiled, pleased that he had called her by her first name. "I have my father's rifle, and I'm a very good shot, if I say so myself."

He shook his head. "I still can't believe that you and your mother live here all alone, with no help and no men to protect you."

She shrugged. "Our men were sacrificed for the war," she replied, then hated herself for the remark when she saw his eyes darken. "I'm sorry," she said.

Her words hung heavily in the air. Grace knew she was behaving badly, but she couldn't seem to help herself.

"I'll go out and have a look."

"I hope you can find what you need," she called pleasantly, hoping to offset her bitter words.

He turned, and their gazes locked for a moment before he nodded and walked out.

Grace stared after him, touched again by his kindness. Something mean in her spirit prompted her to keep making snide little remarks. At first she had even tried to dislike him, but he made that difficult by not taking offense to the bitter words that kept popping out of her mouth. He was a true gentleman who seemed intent on helping them any way he could.

She moved about the kitchen, automatically assembling what she needed to make biscuits. All the while, she stared into space, seeing nothing but Jonathan Parker in her mind's eye. She had never met anyone like him. The local boys had never appealed to her. They had always seemed to be badly in need of learning the basics of etiquette. This was the South, where everyone cut their teeth on being a lady or a gentleman. Before the war, the young men thought of nothing but racing horses, playing pranks, and trying to hold their liquor, and not doing a very good job at any of it, in her opinion.

She rolled out the dough and turned a cup over to cut out biscuits.

A movement beyond the kitchen window caught her eye. Jonathan Parker was carrying a few tools that looked as rusty as she had feared. Yet there was a lilt to his step and a pleasant expression on his face.

Grace stared at him, unable to resist watching his every move when he was unaware of her. He walked with a long purposeful stride, as though he always knew exactly where he was going and what he was doing.

As he disappeared around the side of the house, Grace thought about how eagerly he had spoken of his farm in Kentucky and his desire to restock cattle and horses.

She swallowed hard, not wanting to hope or dream, but she couldn't help herself. She was only nineteen years old, yet she felt at least the age of Agnes, the spinster neighbor, who was thirty-one and had had no offers of marriage.

Grace bit her lip as the frustration of her endless conflict gripped her again. No matter how many times she reminded herself that it did no good to wail about life not being fair, at times like this she wanted to scream at the top of her lungs about how cheated and disheartened she felt.

Why did she have to live out her life at Riverwood with a mother whom she loved dearly but who seemed determined to live in the past?

She grabbed up the bread pan, dipped into her lard bowl, and swabbed the pan generously. Then she began to place each biscuit onto the greased pan.

A fierce ache squeezed her throat, and she swallowed hard against it. She would not cry over something as silly as a lost dream. A dream was an elusive thing. People were flesh and blood and a part of her soul. She had lost a father and a brother, and now her mother just sat on the front porch and waited for "her Fred" to come home. Grace was left to worry about the neglected farmland that needed to produce crops to pay their taxes and put food on their table. It had taken the kindness of a total stranger to make even the most basic repair: the front gate. Yet that same kindness had strangely twisted her heart, flirting with her, reminding her of how lonely she had been throughout the past years.

She'd be better off not to know that there were men like Jonathan Parker walking the face of the earth, returning to a wonderful life he would share with. . .well, she was sure he had his pick of lovely Kentucky women.

"But I'm not going to think about that," she said aloud. She no longer worried about talking to herself. She had grown to like her own company.

four

"How far is the nearest hardware store?" Jonathan asked as they sat at the table, eating breakfast.

"About three miles down the road at Whites Creek."

He looked from Grace to Elizabeth, who was seated at the head of the table, sipping her coffee, watching Jonathan appreciatively.

"Then I'd like to ride into Whites Creek and pick up a new hammer and some nails. I want you to have a sturdy gate. And you do need some new tools," he added gently.

"How nice of you," Elizabeth smiled.

Grace stared at him. "You don't have to go to that much trouble."

"I insist. If you don't mind, that is."

She shook her head. "No, I don't mind. In fact, I need to make a trip in to pick up some more seeds for my garden. I'll saddle up Molly and tag along."

"Is Molly up to the trip? I noticed she has a limp."

"Oh yes. She's had a limp ever since I've known her. Mr. Douglas loaned her to us because she could no longer pull a wagon or work in the field. But Molly is just fine to ride. As a matter of fact, we get along very well. Next to Mother, Molly is about my best friend," she said with a grin.

He chuckled softly, and Grace's grin deepened into a smile. She liked the sound of his laughter. It was full and deep and exactly the way a person should sound when amused. She had never liked the shallow little laughs of Farrel Watson, down in Whites Creek, who was always trying to flirt with her but never quite figured out how.

41

"Well, I'm glad you and Molly understand one another. I was a little concerned when I fed her this morning."

"Thanks for feeding her." Grace spoke quickly, pleased to have someone to help her. "Then we'll go into Whites Creek. Mother, you need to make a list for me."

Grace watched her mother carefully, wondering if she would object to Grace riding into town with this man whom they scarcely knew.

"All right." Her mother smiled. Grace realized everything had changed. The old rules no longer applied, or at least Grace didn't think so.

Later, dressed in the wrinkled riding habit she had retrieved from the trunk, she met Jonathan in the drive. He had found her old harness and saddle and thoughtfully saddled Molly up, and now they were ready to ride. She watched as he swung onto the big stallion with ease.

"Are you okay?" he asked, looking back over his shoulder as they started off down the drive.

"I'm fine," she called back, silently admiring General, the big stallion, as he pranced down the drive. Feeling disloyal to Molly, she leaned over and stroked her mane.

It was a beautiful spring day. After the storm, the air was lighter and sweeter. The honeysuckle blossoms were in bloom, flavoring the air with their special fragrance.

As they reached the end of the drive, Grace took another look at the pitiful old gate and felt embarrassed. It half hung from the hinges, but there was nothing she could do about it. She would be grateful to Jonathan Parker for repairing it. She looked across at him, ready to express her appreciation, but he was already speaking.

"You're very kind to your mother," he said. "I'm sure these have been difficult years for her. And for you."

"The years have been difficult, not just for us, but for everyone. All anyone thinks about anymore is trying to survive. It's the way of war, I suppose." She glanced at Jonathan. "You must be anxious to see your family."

"Yes, I am. And yet—"

"What is it?"

He was silent for a few moments. Then he looked at her and shrugged. "I guess I'm dreading to see the condition of the farm. I know its been badly neglected, and with everyone gone, I'm not sure it will feel like home anymore."

Grace frowned. This idea was something new to her. She had never left Riverwood except for visits to relatives in other parts of the state when she was small. She cast her gaze out across the oak woods, watching a red-winged blackbird sail to a lower branch. The sound of birdsong filled the air, along with the scent of wildflowers. This was home to her. She tried to imagine how it would be for Jonathan, having been away for so long, then returning to an abandoned home. She lifted her eyes toward the blue skies, admiring the soft puffy clouds skimming about.

She made a promise to herself that she was going to quit complaining so much. In fact, she had begun to feel so good that she now regretted wishing that Jonathan had never come to their door. She was so happy to have a friend and to actually be going someplace, if only to Whites Creek.

She looked up at the man whose horse was a few paces ahead of her. He was a good rider, swaying easily with the horse's gait.

"You ride as though you've spent lots of time in the saddle," she called to him.

"I was in the cavalry. And before the war, we rode horses on the farm."

Her eyes swept up his back, clad in a dark coat, then lingered on the wave of dark hair that brushed his collar.

"I can see this is the heart of cotton country," he said, turning his head to look out across the fields.

"Yes." She followed his gaze to the land bordering the road, land as level as a table, stretching as far as the eye could see.

"This was the Abernathy place," she said.

Just ahead, only a blackened chimney remained of the grand home, a sordid reminder of the war and what it had done to families. There was no point in saying more; it was obvious the big house had been burned to the ground. She noticed that Jonathan was looking at the ugly pile of rubbish that marred the tranquil landscape.

"How did you manage to save your place?" he asked.

She took a deep breath, feeling a deep relief when she thought about what had happened. "We were fortunate. Only a few soldiers came to search our place. Of course, the soldiers had already taken our horses and cattle and the wagon. On their last foray, they realized there was little of value for them, and our farm is smaller than those around us. The officer in charge was a kind, older gentleman who took mercy on Mother and me. They left us alone."

"Thank God," Jonathan said, breathing a deep sigh.

"Yes, Mother thanked God every night after that. And for awhile, I did too. I guess I forget to be grateful."

Beyond the next field, tumbled shanties that had been slave quarters were now rotting wood with birds nesting in the rafters.

"I'm glad the slaves were freed," she said, staring at the dismal reminder of their lives before the war. "I always got into arguments about people owning slaves. Father always hired Irishmen to do our work, once he managed to buy enough land to raise cotton. And Ardella and William were like family. They stayed with us until they both died."

His interest in their home led her thoughts toward his farm in Kentucky. "I do hope you find your farm in good shape when you return to Kentucky," she said. "Perhaps your brother-in-law has seen to it that the farm has been kept up."

He turned his face sideways to answer her. She saw his profile from a different angle and noticed that his nose was perfectly straight. The jaw was broad with prominent bones capping his cheeks.

"I have my doubts about my brother-in-law. James has no interest in the farm. I suspect Mother may have trouble dragging Katherine back to the farm if she's become spoiled to city life. Katie is spoiled anyway, being the baby," he said, chuckling softly.

He hesitated as they rode on. "It's hard to believe that the redheaded pixie I left is now a lady of sixteen. She may even have a beau."

"What does she look like?" Grace asked, curious about his family.

"She's a fiery little redhead given to temper tantrums. I doubt if Mother has managed to curtail that temper through the years. But the war may have changed Katie too." He sighed. "It would really make me sad to return to find my spunky little sister is now a very serious woman."

"She probably has a beau; she may even be married," Grace said. "And I imagine she's very pretty. Are her eyes like yours?" she asked, then wished she hadn't when she heard the admiration in her tone.

Jonathan didn't seem to think anything of the question, however. "As a matter of fact, they're exactly the same color of blue. That's the only resemblance. She has small features and pretty hair, very thick. . .like yours," he added softly.

Grace perked up. Automatically, she lifted a hand to touch a strand of hair curling over the shoulder of her dress. So he had noticed her thick hair, which she always thought was one of her best features. That pleased her.

"What plans do you have for Riverwood?" he asked in a sudden change of subject.

Her thoughts moved back to the home she loved. She couldn't imagine being separated from it, as Jonathan had been. "Well," she began, then paused to ponder her future. "The main thing is to keep the taxes paid so that carpetbaggers don't buy our land for next to nothing." She shook her head, recalling the horrible stories she had heard. "With Confederate money worthless, and no way to make money on the land, it's very difficult to pay the taxes; but if they're not paid, the land can be sold off for as little as a dollar an acre. My father and Mr. Britton, the banker, were best friends, and because of that, Mr. Britton has been generous and patient."

Grace pressed her lips together to keep from saying more. The truth was Mr. Britton was having financial problems himself. He couldn't afford to keep holding her note. She would have to figure out a way to pay him back by the end of the year.

"You mentioned that a neighbor married for the sake of the family, to extend the land lines—I believe that's the way you put it. I imagine you have been presented with offers."

Grace shrugged. "I would never marry for that reason."

"May I ask why not?"

"Because I will never marry unless I truly love the man."

"You seem quite certain of that," he said, tilting his head sideways again, as though trying to read her expression.

"I am. And furthermore, it won't be easy for a man to live with me."

He chuckled at that remark. "And may I ask why you would say something like that?"

She smiled to herself, remembering an old argument. "Father used to say, 'Grace, with that strong personality, you'll never find a man who can live with you.'" She gave a short laugh and looked out across the barren fields. "It was my thirteenth birthday, and I had thrown a temper tantrum because

Mother insisted on a tea party to celebrate my birthday. What I really wanted to do was go with Father to Tuscaloosa to a horse-and-cattle auction."

"At thirteen you wanted to do that?" he asked, laughing.

She thought he seemed overly amused at her honest statements, but she took it good-naturedly. "I hoped to talk Father into buying me a fine horse," she explained. "I had already chosen a name. Darkfire."

"So what happened?"

"Father agreed with Mother, and I had to endure a silly tea party. I never got the kind of horse I wanted."

"Well, I'll bet your father was secretly proud of your spirit. I think it's admirable for a woman to be a bit independent."

She was pleased by that remark, one so different than she would have heard from most of the boys she had known. They would expect her to be meek and mealy-mouthed like—

She broke off her train of thought, reminding herself not to be unkind about Agnes.

"I was independent for sure," she said, laughing with him. It occurred to her that it was good to hear the sound of her own laughter ringing in her ears.

They rode on in silence, and Grace relished the smell of wildflowers and the feel of a horse moving beneath her. Having Jonathan Parker riding in front of her was no hardship. She sighed to herself. This was turning into a perfect day.

All too soon they were approaching Whites Creek, so she sat up straight and thought about what she had to do.

The main street was flanked by twin rows of small wooden shops with oak trees behind them for shade. Long wooden hitching rails paralleled the front of each shop, and Grace counted three sorrels and two bays tied out front. A fancy buggy was parked in front of the general store, and further down the street near the livery, she saw a team of mules and an old wagon.

Along the uneven boards that served as walkways, a few women, in dark calico and frayed sunbonnets, sauntered along, their market baskets swinging from their arms.

"The general store is the second building there," she pointed.

As they turned toward the hitching rail in front of the store, Grace was suddenly aware of bold stares sweeping over her. Across the street at the livery, a stranger had appeared beside the wagon. He stood with his hands on his hips, his eyes narrowed on Jonathan.

Grace glanced away, scanning the boardwalk again. She recognized the faces of some of the merchants, peering from doorways, but they were not smiling at her.

Mrs. Primrose, who helped her husband at the store, was crossing the street from the bank. A look of curiosity worked over her face as she stepped into the street and struck a path toward Grace.

Jonathan had dismounted and had extended his hand to help Grace down. She had a sudden urge to refuse his help, knowing that Mrs. Primrose was trained on her like a hawk swooping down on its prey. Looking into Jonathan's nice eyes, however, Grace took his hand and dismounted.

"Grace?" Mrs. Primrose yelled, trying to catch up. "How is your mother?"

Grace took a deep breath and forced a smile as she turned to face the older woman, who wasn't even looking at her. The beady eyes studied Jonathan, taking in every detail.

"She's all right, Mrs. Primrose."

Grace was about to turn in spite of the fact that the woman stood directly in their path, still staring at Jonathan.

Grace averted her eyes to her riding skirt, brushing it carefully as though too preoccupied to introduce her traveling companion.

Jonathan merely tipped his hat, saying nothing, for which

Grace was thankful. She dared not introduce him, for if he opened his mouth and Mrs. Primrose caught one Yankee syllable, she might flog both of them.

Jonathan seemed to understand as he fell in step beside her, and they stepped up onto the boards leading into the general store. Glancing over her shoulder, Grace saw Mrs. Primrose turn to speak to a couple passing by in a wagon.

"I'll do the talking," she said, under her breath.

She had hoped the beautiful day would send everyone to their fields and gardens, but many had chosen to make the trip to town to restock supplies.

The smell of leather and plug tobacco was strong as the door of the general store swung back at Jonathan's touch. In the rear, seated on upturned nail kegs, Grace spotted several men she recognized. They were huddled up around the hearth. In winter, the hearth at the general store was the meeting place for drinking coffee and swapping tales. There was no fire in the hearth today; still they sat and talked. One of the men, wearing the gray trousers of his uniform, was heatedly relating a story to the others.

"The Yanks took all our horses, our mules, the brass-trimmed carriage, and ever' last wagon we had. They raided the smokehouse and pantry and left us nothing. Had three bales of cotton down in the shed—"

He stopped in midsentence as all the men noticed Grace and Jonathan. From the corner of her eye, she could see all heads swivel toward her, then Jonathan. She lifted her chin and headed toward the counter. "I need a hammer and some nails," she said as Mr. Primrose walked up to the counter. "And do you have any tomato plants?"

"None today," he said, looking from Grace to Jonathan, taking him in from hat to boot. "Could I help you, Sir?"

"He's with me," Grace answered quickly.

Everyone in the store was looking and listening now. She

stole a glance at Jonathan and saw that his expression was solemn. He pursed his lips and looked around, meeting each stare directly. Nodding briefly at those who were gawking, he turned to Grace.

She breathed a sigh of relief until her supplies were spread over the counter. Grace froze. There was no point in reaching into her handbag; she hadn't enough money to cover the purchase. She could feel the blood rise to her cheeks as she stared at the sturdy new hammer, unsure what to do next.

Jonathan had wandered over to a shelf where jars of homemade pickles and relishes had been placed with a sign that read PLEASE HELP THE WIDOWS OF THE CONFEDERACY. Jonathan removed a jar of each and returned to the counter.

Mr. Primrose totaled the bill and announced the amount. Saying nothing, Jonathan placed some money on the counter. Mr. Primrose examined the newly minted bills, looking pleased.

"Thank you, Sir," he said, looking at Jonathan.

Jonathan nodded as he picked up the package, and they headed for the door. Grace felt the boards vibrate beneath her feet as Sonny Jackson lumbered up to her. He must have been hunkered down somewhere in the back of the store, for she hadn't seen him before. If she had known the town bully was lurking about, she would never have entered the store. Sonny spent his time looking for someone to pester, hoping to stir up a fight.

His pale, watery blue eyes were set between straggly brown brows and thick cheeks. Thin brown hair straggled down from his soiled derby hat, and as usual, his clothes were wrinkled and soiled, though he no longer worked in the fields.

"Hello, Miss Grace. You and yore ma doin' all right?" He stood beside the door, his fat thumbs hooked into the loops of his belt.

"We're fine," she said curtly, sidestepping him as Jonathan

reached out to open the door.

"As a friend of Freddy's, I hafta look out for his little sis. Who's your fancy friend here?" He had followed them out onto the sidewalk and was standing directly in front of Jonathan, making a show of looking over Jonathan's frock coat and pinstriped trousers.

"Sonny, I think you need to mind your own business," Grace said. "You and Freddy were never friends; in fact, he hated your guts."

She could have bitten her tongue once the words were out, for this was all Sonny needed to urge him on.

"Yeah, well I still say Freddy would want me lookin' after his kin. Don't believe I ever seen you around these parts, Mister."

"You wouldn't have seen me unless you were a soldier in the army," Jonathan said coldly, glaring into Sonny's eyes. "And I doubt that you were." He was taller than Sonny by three or four inches, and the fact that he could look down on Sonny seemed to gall the bully even more.

Sonny sputtered for a moment before muttering a curse and diving into Jonathan's chest. He caught Jonathan off guard. Jonathan's hat toppled, and the package in his arms spurted from his grip as he was knocked back against the door.

Grace dived for the package, then reached for his hat. Like bees to a hive, a crowd was gathering, whispering among themselves. "A Yankee," someone muttered.

Grace took a firmer grip on Jonathan's hat and their package and yelled at Sonny. "Stop it," she cried, just before Jonathan ducked beneath Sonny's swinging fist.

Moving with the grace of a cat, Jonathan sidestepped him, then slammed a fist in the center of Sonny's sagging belly. Sonny groaned and bent double, his arms swinging wildly.

In the next instant, Jonathan's arm shot out again. His fist caught Sonny on the chin, and the bully reeled back. He landed in the street, doubled over, an expression of disbelief on his face.

The men raised their voices, urging Sonny to get up. Grace hurried to Jonathan's side, handing him his hat. "Please, let's get out of here."

Then Ned Whitworth stepped around the corner, and Grace had never in her life been so glad to see the stern sheriff. He stepped in front of Jonathan, whose eyes were narrowed on Sonny. Grace could see that Jonathan was ready to finish the fight. She turned to the sheriff, tugging his sleeve.

"Sheriff, this man is a family friend and—"

"A Yank," someone snorted.

"A no-good, slimy Union soldier," another joined in.

"Stop it!" Sheriff Whitworth snapped at the crowd. "If Miss Grace says he's a friend of hers, then you people better mind your manners."

Sonny was stumbling up, swiping a fat lip with the back of his hand.

"Ned, he started it."

"That's a lie." Jonathan glared at him, doubling his fist again. Then he took a deep breath, as though trying to calm himself as he dropped his hand to his side. "Sheriff, I didn't start this fight, but I won't run from it either."

The sheriff looked into Jonathan's eyes, glanced at Grace, then regarded Jonathan again, nodding his head. "I believe you. But the fight's over." He glanced over his shoulder as Sonny moved behind him. "Don't take another step," he warned. "Or you'll be charged and taken to jail."

Sonny was sputtering with rage, but the sheriff ignored him.

Grace looked from Sonny to the sheriff, then the crowd. She was furious that Jonathan had been treated so rudely, and she was determined to get a word in.

"This man saved my father's life," she said. "He took him to a hospital and befriended him before he died. You should be ashamed of yourselves, all of you!"

Jonathan had taken his hat and the package from her. Placing a hand on her elbow, he walked her back to the horse.

Sheriff Whitworth followed and stood beside them as they mounted their horses.

"Thank you, Sir," Jonathan said, turning to the sheriff.

"Don't judge everyone here by Sonny," Sheriff Whitworth said to Jonathan. "Fred Cunningham was a fine man and respected by everyone who knew him. I'm glad to know that someone repaid his kindness."

Grace smiled at the sheriff, appreciating his words more than he could possibly know. "Thank you."

Then they turned their horses around and rode out of Whites Creek without a backward glance.

five

Jonathan had said nothing in the hour since they had left Whites Creek. When Grace could stand the silence no longer, she spoke up.

"Let's rest a minute."

He nodded and pointed to a grove of oaks near the road. When they had reached the trees, Jonathan swung down from the saddle. Grace let him help her down, although she could have managed on her own. But she was beginning to enjoy the feel of his arms about her, and she liked the consideration he showed her.

He took off his hat and hooked it onto the saddle horn as he picked up the horses' reins and led them toward a hickory sapling. Grace removed her hat and adjusted the hairpins in her chignon. Then she walked over and sank onto the grass, enjoying the cool shade. She felt hot and parched and thoroughly out of sorts.

"I forgot to offer you water," Jonathan said. "I drew fresh water from your well before I left," he explained, removing the lid from a canteen. He handed her the canteen and sat down beside her.

Grace drank greedily of the cool water. When she had finished she handed the canteen back to him. He reached out, and for a moment, his hand lingered on hers.

"Thank you," she said softly.

"You're welcome."

His gaze trailed down her nose and rested for a moment on her lips. The pine scent that seemed so much a part of him touched her, and it was hard to determine if it were the man or the deep woods nearby that captured her senses. Her glance swept the smooth curve of his chin, then moved up his slim nose to the eyes, which he closed as he drank the water. She could see that he was as thirsty as she.

Aware that she was staring, she turned and looked out across the landscape. A doe stood at the edge of the woods, its ears perked. Something moved behind the doe, something small and light brown. The doe had a little one.

"I'm sorry," Jonathan said, breaking into her thoughts.

She leaned back on her arms and looked across at him. A worried frown creased his brow, and his eyes were troubled.

"For what?" she asked.

"For brawling with that idiot when I knew better."

"You put him in his place," she countered, thinking how she had respected his actions, once she had had time to think about them.

"It was a mistake. It will give some of them a reason to hate me more. And I don't want anyone bothering you after I'm gone."

"After you're gone," she echoed, then caught herself. She looked back toward the woods, hoping to see the doe again. She didn't want to think about Jonathan leaving. Not now.

"I'll be leaving soon," he said, as though to emphasize his point.

"Why?" She looked into his eyes and felt her heart quicken. She didn't know if it was his kindness to her dying father or his gentleness with her mother, but something about Jonathan made it easy to love him. Despite the fact that he was a Yankee. She swallowed and began again. "There's no hurry. You don't have to leave after you repair the gate. And you don't have to fix the gate, you know."

"I want to. But. . ."

"But what?" She searched his face, longing to read his mind, to know exactly what he was thinking.

Without looking at her, he stood up and gazed at something in the distance. "It wouldn't be a good idea for me to stay any longer. You see the hostility people feel toward me."

She thought about that. "But it would probably be the same if I were visiting in your area."

He reached out a hand to help her up. A wry grin touched the corners of his mouth. "You're too pretty to pick on."

"You know what I mean." She grinned, still holding his hand.

"I'm not sure of anything anymore," he said, squeezing her hand. "I do know that you and I live in different worlds. Still. . ." He turned, leading the way back to the horse as they held hands. "Still, I'm glad we met," he said as she leaned against him to place her foot in the stirrup.

Because she was a bundle of nerves, her boot slipped out of the stirrup, and she lunged even closer to him. The arms that had steadied her pulled her closer. She tilted her head back to look into his face. His blue eyes captured her, and she felt her senses whirling. She moved closer to him, wanting him to kiss her, hoping he would.

He hesitated for a moment, as though reluctant, but then he lowered his head, and his lips brushed hers, gently, sweetly. The kiss lasted only a moment, yet time seemed to stand still for Grace. She had never before felt such sweet longing. But Jonathan's blue eyes deepened, and he turned toward the stirrup, holding it firmly.

Taking the hint, she placed her boot firmly in the stirrup and swung herself into the saddle. He gathered up the reins, stroked his horse's neck for a second, then mounted.

Nothing was said as they rode back to Riverwood. Grace stared at the barren fields bordering the road, but she was no longer thinking of the doe and the little one, or the landscape, or the war, or anything else. Something was happening between Jonathan and her, and she was afraid to think about it. She told herself not to get serious about him, but her heart refused to listen. She was falling in love with him, and she knew it; worse, she couldn't seem to help herself.

"Your mother is sitting out on the porch," Jonathan said as they rode up the driveway.

"Yes, I suppose she'll go on sitting out there every afternoon, reading the Bible and hoping Father will magically appear."

She studied her mother, sitting very still in the cane-backed rocker, her little face tilted toward them. Grace was amazed at how peaceful her mother looked. Grace rarely felt at peace, and she certainly could not sit still long enough to loiter on the porch.

"Maybe she's only waiting for us," she said, hoping that at last her mother had decided to accept the sad truth.

Jonathan pulled the reins back on his horse and alighted from the saddle, and again she let him help her down. *Might as well enjoy it while I can,* she thought, stealing a look at him. Their eyes met and held, and she remembered the kiss and looked nervously at her mother.

Once Jonathan had helped her down and she'd brushed off her skirt, she stole another glance at her mother, whose smile was still in place.

"Mother, we got what we needed," Grace called, walking up the steps to the porch. She glanced over her shoulder, watching Jonathan remove their package from his saddlebag. "And Jonathan bought some jars of pickles and relish that the Confederate widows are selling."

He approached the steps, looking a bit embarrassed by her compliments.

"That was a very nice thing to do, by the way," Grace added.

"Would you two like to sit on the porch for awhile? Grace, you could make some lemonade." The older woman looked from Grace back to Jonathan. "I sit here every day, waiting—"

"Mother. . .you know what Jonathan came to tell us," Grace said, beginning to feel exasperated by her mother's behavior. "You have to accept the truth. Father is not coming home."

Elizabeth shook her head, her eyes still focused on the driveway. "God has assured me Fred will come home."

"Mother, stop it!" Grace cried out. "Please don't do this. You're only hurting yourself. And you're hurting me."

Her mother acted as though she had not heard her daughter's anguished words. She said nothing, yet she never stopped scanning the driveway.

Grace fought back tears of frustration. She whirled to Jonathan, who had climbed the porch steps and stood at a distance, looking slightly embarrassed.

"Jonathan, tell her Father is dead, that he isn't coming home."

His blue eyes darkened as he looked from Grace to her mother. For a moment, he seemed to be locked in an inner conflict over what to say. Then he looked back at Grace. "I can't say for sure that he is never coming back, Grace."

Grace glared at him. "What do you mean? You came all this way to bring the Bible, to tell us he was dying."

"Yes, he was dying. But he was alive when I left, and even though I doubt he could have lasted long, I can't say for sure that your father is dead."

"Don't do this!" she lashed out at him. "Of course he is dead. If not, we would have heard from him. Father had an iron will; I know that. If he had any hope of living, he would not have sent you here." Tears were streaming down her cheeks, tears of anger and hopelessness borne from having to endure so much heartache.

"Fred will come back to me," her mother said softly from behind them. "In the meantime, I will cling to my faith, and I will wait for him."

come back and have a bite to eat before you leave. Fred would not want you to leave our home without a gracious good-bye. I'll expect to see you back." Her voice was firm, and Grace could only stare at her. It was as though her mother had suddenly emerged as the woman she had once been. For a moment Grace believed that she was as sane as ever, that she only escaped to her world of fantasy to hide from her heartbreak.

"Thank you, Mrs. Cunningham. I'll do that."

Without a glance toward the stairs, Jonathan hurried up the hall.

Grace turned and flew up the stairs. She had to get to her room fast. Her mother's words had drained the anger from Grace's soul, and she was stung by the reprimand. In the depths of her conscience, she regretted the words she had spoken to Jonathan. Even more, she was sorry her mother had heard what she had said about her. Her mother was like a fragile little bird with a broken wing; Grace had no right to be cruel to her. For all of Mother's talk about faith, God hadn't changed things, after all. He had merely shown her someone she could never have for her own.

Grace trudged into her room to change clothes. She still had time to work in the garden, and it always calmed her down to put her hands in the soil. She would stay busy out back, avoiding Jonathan Parker. After he repaired the gate and came back for his horse, she wouldn't have to speak to him again. And she would be glad when he was gone.

She grabbed up some clean work clothes and changed out of her riding habit. As she dressed, her mother's words continued to haunt her.

"Just forget it," Grace snapped to herself. She took a deep breath and made her way outside to the row of beans. At least there was plenty to keep her busy.

An hour later, she heard a familiar voice. "Miss Grace?"

She turned to see Reams standing at the corner of the house, holding a small brown sack. He wore faded overalls and a clean gray shirt, and below his felt hat, silver hair framed his dark face and highlighted large dark eyes. He grinned, warming Grace's heart.

"Hi, Reams." She dusted her hands on her overalls and walked up to the backyard. "How's Chloe?"

"She's her usual cantankerous self," he said chuckling. He and his wife adored one another even though they constantly teased. "Sent you some fresh eggs. You know, Mr. Douglas bought more hens."

"How thoughtful of you. Come on inside. It's time for me to take a break."

"Yes'm. I was just talking with that fella down there fixing your fence. He seems mighty nice."

Grace lowered her eyes as her conscience indicted her once again. "He saved Father's life," she said, leading the way to the house.

"Yes'm. I spoke to Miss Lizbeth on the front porch. She told me about it. Said she was about to make him some lunch."

Grace could hear the clatter of dishes from the kitchen and guessed her mother was already preparing the food. "Why don't you stay and eat with us?"

"I reckon Mr. Douglas won't mind."

"Of course not," she called over her shoulder. Reams and Chloe had been at Oak Grove for over twenty years. They were treated like family and had no desire to leave.

As she scraped her boots on the back doorstep, she heard her mother talking, then she heard Jonathan's deep voice. She hesitated. Reams was coming up the steps behind her, and she remembered she had invited him to lunch. She wasn't going to hide down in the garden as though she were afraid to face him, so squaring her shoulders she led the way into the kitchen.

Her mother was pouring coffee for Jonathan. He sat at the trestle table with a plate of biscuits and preserves.

"Reams is going to join us." Grace spoke quickly, trying to cover her embarrassment about her treatment of Jonathan.

"Good. Have a seat, Reams." Jonathan said, avoiding Grace's eyes as well.

Reams settled down on the bench beside Jonathan.

"I was just relating a story that Mr. Cunningham told me about crossing the Warrior River back during flood days. He was a very brave man," Jonathan said, looking at Reams.

"Yes, Sir, he was," Reams said. "And Mr. Fred was a good man. I feel sorry for you, Miss Elizabeth. And for you, Miss Grace."

Grace turned and smiled at Reams. "We're managing." Then she turned to finish washing her hands, wishing she hadn't sounded so defensive.

"We are grateful to Jonathan for traveling a long way on a mission from Fred," Elizabeth said. She had not poured coffee for herself, nor was she eating anything.

"Yes'm," Reams said quietly.

A moment of silence hung over them as everyone suddenly seemed at a loss of words. Then Reams cleared his throat and nodded. "Sir, could I ask you something?"

"Sure."

Grace poured herself half a cup of coffee. After rationing themselves on coffee for so long, it still seemed wasteful to have more than one cup a day. But this was a special occasion, she told herself, sneaking a glance toward the table where the men sat.

"Well," Reams continued slowly, "we being admirers of President Lincoln, we been grieving about the assassination. What do you know of the man who shot him?"

"Oh, you mean John Wilkes Booth." For the second time since she had known him, Grace watched Jonathan's jaw clench in anger. "Booth was a madman who professed loyalty to the South, although he was never loyal enough to join the Confederate Army. He had a burning hatred of slavery and of Abraham Lincoln. I've heard that he had concocted some wild scheme to kidnap President Lincoln and take him to Richmond with the intention of exchanging him for prisoners. But then he decided to kill the president instead."

Silence settled over the kitchen as everyone listened to Jonathan. Grace found herself admiring his intelligence and his strong, yet gentle spirit. She had never met anyone like this man, and she was feeling terrible about what she'd said to him. She didn't want him to leave. Not yet. But how could she keep him here? What could she possibly say or do to change his mind when he was determined to go?

"Reams, Mr. Cunningham told me he had never owned slaves, that he never would. He said he employed Irishmen to work the fields. Where did these men go?"

Reams sat back and shook his head. "I don't rightly know."

Grace spoke up. "Once Father left, they scattered. I think some joined the army; others went to seek relatives. None are in the county. I wish they were," she said, taking her seat on the bench opposite the men.

No one spoke for a few minutes, as they drank their coffee and pondered the nation's plight. Then Jonathan spoke up again. "I know there are men who need work. If we could get a few good men to clear some of your fields and plant cotton—"

"But we have no money to pay them," Grace said.

Reams sighed and looked from Grace to Elizabeth. "I'd better be going." He stood up slowly and Jonathan extended his hand.

"It was nice meeting you," he said to Reams.

"Will you be staying a few days?" Reams asked.

"I've asked him to please stay another day," Elizabeth

spoke up, her voice soft and gentle.

Grace stole a glance at Jonathan and saw that he was watching her reaction to the news. She realized that her mother and even Reams were looking at her as well. She fiddled with a strand of hair brushing her cheek. She didn't know how to backtrack on her order for him to leave. Then Reams spoke up, saving her from an awkward situation.

"You were asking about help here. I'd been thinking of riding over to see two of my cousins at Jina. Mr. Douglas could use two more hands, and maybe they could kind of help out."

"Good idea," Jonathan said. "Reams, what do you think could be grown here on a small scale?"

Reams hesitated, looking from Jonathan to Grace and back again. "Lots of folks is planting corn. It don't bring what cotton did, but it's cheap enough to plant and tend. And I could help out. Mr. Douglas would let me do that, I reckon."

"How kind of both of you." Elizabeth turned to them, a new light shining in the hazel eyes that had so often looked weary and distracted.

"Corn," Jonathan said, grinning as though he remembered something.

"What are you thinking?" Grace asked.

"I was just thinking of all the times as a soldier I would go into a corn field and get half-ripened corn and eat it to keep going."

"Half-ripened corn?" Grace stared at him.

He nodded. "Believe me, if you're hungry enough, it isn't bad. In fact, I preferred it over flour and water fried in lard. That was our meal many nights. I watched one soldier eat a bullfrog," he said, making a face.

"Ain't bad," Reams said, chuckling. "I've eaten a few frog legs in my day. Quite tasty."

Suddenly they were all smiling and laughing with Reams. Grace felt the tension from their argument slipping away as she met Jonathan's gaze, and he smiled at her.

Then Jonathan turned and looked at Reams. "You have a good idea about growing corn. Let's see what we can do about that." He looked back at Grace and smiled.

As Grace returned his smile, she considered his offer of helping to get some corn planted. If he wanted to do them a favor, why not let him?

"Since I haven't finished with the gate, I'd better get back to work," Jonathan said, standing up.

"And I'd better get back to the garden," Grace said.

"And this evening I'll prepare the meal," Elizabeth announced, smiling at Grace.

Grace smiled back, pleased to see her mother being active again. Jonathan whistled as he went out the back door. And as Grace returned to the garden, she felt a sense of relief that she had not experienced in a very long time.

six

After supper, Elizabeth suggested they sit out on the porch. It seemed to be the place where she was happiest, and Grace and Jonathan thought it a good idea.

They sat on the front porch for an hour, talking in generalities. Elizabeth asked Jonathan about Kentucky, and he spoke fondly of his home, giving them an interesting look at another part of the country. No reference was made to the war.

When Elizabeth decided to go in, Jonathan looked at Grace. It was obvious he was unsure if he should stay with Grace or go inside.

"We can sit out for awhile longer, if you want," Grace said.

He smiled and leaned back in his chair. Neither spoke. Grace suspected he was still feeling awkward about their argument, and she decided it was time to make her peace.

"I'm sorry about today. I. . .regret what I said to you."

He was thoughtful for a moment. "It's okay."

Silence stretched between them again, and Grace felt compelled to explain her position a bit more. "I just get tired of wishing that Mother could accept reality. Father isn't coming home, and we have to accept that and go on with our lives."

"I can understand how you feel about that. Yet I'm fascinated by your mother's strength. I believe she's in full command of her senses, Grace. I've had the opportunity to spend some time with her, and I sincerely believe that she needs to think about your father returning in order to cope with the. . . loss. She believes there is still some hope, and who's to say she isn't right?"

Grace felt a tug of war starting in her heart. "But I can't

feel that way, don't you see? It's as though we never get out of the past, but we have to move on, even though we hate what has happened."

"I understand, and I think you are very brave."

She sighed. "Oh Jonathan, I'm not that brave. I'm just like thousands of women who are trying to survive. We go on because we have no choice. As for Mother and her faith. . ." She paused, thinking.

"Mother clings to her faith, spending hours with the Bible and trying to get me to do the same. But God and I have had a falling out. He doesn't seem to be listening to our prayers. I can understand Him not paying attention to mine, for I've been rebellious and sassy. But my folks have always been very religious, attending church. They even helped build a church up on Sand Mountain before we moved here. Why has God let all these terrible things happen to our family?"

"Grace, as you said a few minutes ago, thousands of women have endured the kind of tragedy you and your mother are facing. Some women have lost their husbands and their sons. It's happened in the North as well as here. Who can explain it? As human beings, we have no answers. To me, it seems useless to try and figure it out."

She looked across at him, studying his chiseled features in the moonlight. She knew what he was saying made sense, that he was probably right, but it didn't make her feel better. Yet in another way, she did feel better.

"Thanks for listening to me," she said. "It helps to talk. I know that. There just hasn't been anyone to say these things to because I sound so bitter. And you're right; everyone has suffered from the war."

He turned and smiled at her. Though nothing was said, it seemed they had made their peace and learned more about each other in the process.

This silence between them was peaceful. A light breeze

stirred through the trees, and a full moon poured silver light across the landscape.

"It's beautiful here," Jonathan said, staring out at the trees.

"I do love it," Grace replied. "Even though I do a lot of fussing, it doesn't really mean I don't love Riverwood. I'm as tied to the land as Father and Freddy were."

"When you speak of them, I can see that you remember happy times."

She nodded. "Good family times. I'm grateful we had that." She looked across at him, thinking again how nice it was to have someone to talk to, someone like Jonathan, who was kind and sympathetic.

"And you should be grateful," he said. "During the war, I met all kinds of men. Sadly, some seemed to have no attachment to home and family; others were planning to go out West rather than return to the homes they had left before the war."

Grace was curious about his part in the war. She hadn't wanted to ask earlier, for she didn't want to think about him fighting on the opposite side. But he had shown only kindness to her family, and she was grateful he had survived.

"When did you join the army? And where did you fight?"

Even in the shadows, she could see her questions had startled him, but he did not hesitate in answering.

"I joined the Union Army after the Battle of Bull Run."

There was no need to ask why. Grace knew the Confederates had won the Battle of Bull Run, or Manassas as Southerners called it.

"I think the North was shocked by that victory," he continued. "People realized this was going to be a difficult war. At first, I didn't want to be a soldier." He spoke slowly, looking out into the darkness. "I hated the idea of fighting in a war where family members actually fought each other. We had heard of this with our neighbors who had just settled in Kentucky from Georgia. They knew they would be fighting their cousins." He leaned his head back against the chair and closed his eyes. "But I had no choice. I had to defend my beliefs."

As she listened to him, she began to see the war through the eyes of someone on the other side. He had not wanted to go to war, nor had he rushed in at the very beginning, as Freddy had. She shook her head and closed her eyes. "What a long, pitiful battle it was—for everyone."

They sat in silence. Only the distant call of a whippoorwill filled the moonlit night. Grace opened her eyes and saw that Jonathan had stood up and was reaching for her hand. "You are an amazing woman. You've been so strong for your mother. I know it's been difficult."

"Yes," she whispered, stepping closer to him. She was hoping he would kiss her again and they could stop talking about sad things. There had been enough sadness in their lives. She tilted her head back and looked up into his face, wondering why he didn't kiss her.

"Grace," he said gently, "I like you very much, more than I want to think about. But we can't feel this way. There is no future."

She caught her breath. Her mind rushed for words, but she could find none. She wished he wouldn't try to be so sensible. Maybe there was no future, but they still had the present. And she so wanted to be happy for a change.

"You're much too serious," she whispered, searching his eyes for hope. She found none.

"I have to be serious when I know the facts. There is so much bitterness, so much hatred. We both saw it today."

"I don't care," she cried. "I just want to be happy."

"So do I," he said, dropping her hand. "But we each have to find happiness in a different way. I have to return to Kentucky."

"Why do you keep reminding me?" she lashed out. "You seem to want to be miserable and to keep me that way. Can't you forget for a moment all the sad terrible things out there? Can't you look at me and pretend to care about me?"

"I don't have to pretend," he said huskily, staring down into her face.

It was all the encouragement she needed. She stood on tip-toe and kissed his lips, and in a moment he was responding. His arms circled her waist and pulled her closer as the kiss deepened. He pulled away, shaking his head.

"I can't do this. I'm older than you, and after all I've witnessed the past four years, I should know better than to hope for anything between a Northern man and a Southern woman."

But Grace smiled. In her heart she knew she was going to change his mind about everything. She loved him, and it was only a matter of time until he admitted that he loved her too.

seven

When Grace awoke the next morning, the sunlight streamed over her bed, and a bird sang sweetly outside her window. Her first thought as her eyes opened to a new day was Jonathan Parker.

He was a wonderful man, she decided. Then she remembered the way he had kissed her. A lazy grin crossed her face, and she shivered with delight. She doubted that she would ever forget that kiss. And she would probably never enjoy another kiss as much. She nestled into the pillow, relishing the memory of standing with him in the moonlight, feeling the tingle of first love from her head to her toes.

"So that's what love is all about," she said to herself, and a feeling of joy flowed through her. She had heard girls talk about being in love, but she had given up all hope of it ever happening to her. Now it had.

She sat up in bed and peered into the mirror. Her thick blond hair was tousled about her face, but her eyes were wide open and glowing like the full moon last night. That silly little smile kept tugging her lips up. She was pleased with her reflection as she turned and tossed the covers back and padded barefoot to the washstand.

Later, when she sauntered down the stairs to investigate the whereabouts of Jonathan Parker, she found her mother in the kitchen, puttering around the pantry.

"Good morning, Mother."

Her mother peered around the pantry door. "Hello, Dear," she smiled. "He's down there fixing the gate."

"Already?" she frowned, wondering if he had slept at all.

"Dear, it's nine o'clock. You really slept late." Her mother smiled at her. "Are you hungry?"

Grace spotted some leftover biscuits on the cabinet, along with the pot of coffee. "I'm so grateful for coffee," she said, remembering how it had been rationed during the war. They still were unable to buy sugar.

"I could smell the coffee when I came downstairs. Jonathan was sitting out on the porch, drinking coffee and eating a biscuit." She paused, looking at Grace and smiling. "I guess he likes your biscuits."

Grace merely grinned as she reached down to pluck a fat brown biscuit from the plate. "I like them too," she said. Then she reached for a mug and poured herself a cup of coffee.

Elizabeth had emerged from the pantry with a pan of potatoes and a paring knife. "I'm going to start lunch."

"Thanks," Grace said, biting into her biscuit. She was relieved to see her mother busy. Some days all she did was read her Bible and stare out the window.

Finishing her biscuit, Grace sipped her coffee and wandered toward the front door. Pushing it open, she stepped out onto the porch and sat down in the chair. As she did, her eyes lingered on the spot where Jonathan had kissed her. She felt as though she had swallowed all the silver light of the moon from the night before.

She sat back in the chair and looked down the driveway. She could hear the sound of the hammer pelting wood as Jonathan worked on the gate. Then Grace frowned. What would happen when the gate was fixed?

Grace's thoughts hung in suspension for a moment. Then his words from the evening before filled her mind. *We have to find happiness in a different way. . . . I have to return to Kentucky.*

Her eyes closed with pain. She would think of something to detain him. She needed him here. His family was managing their lives without him; his father had died before the war began. And he had said his mother and his sister would want to stay in Louisville.

She opened her eyes, feeling better. Suddenly she remembered what he had said to Reams. He had asked about finding someone to help Grace and her mother. A pleased little smile tilted her lips. Mr. Jonathan Parker might find out that obtaining farm help would not be so easy, after all. She had heard Mr. Douglas complaining about how difficult it was for him to find field hands.

She frowned. If they did find someone to work, how was she supposed to pay them?

She stood up and began to pace the porch. For a minute she almost wished they could stay in the stalemate they were in, just to keep Jonathan with them. Yet she knew they had to get on with their lives. That meant she needed help in getting the land cleared and replanted. After all, there was a limit to how long Mr. Britton would wait on his loan, and she and her mother couldn't depend on their little garden to feed them forever.

Grace paced back and forth, seriously concerned. She hated having to be the head of the house, worrying about all the decisions that a man should rightfully make. She wanted to be a woman in love with a man; she wanted to think about marriage and a family. Her pacing stopped as she reached the end of the porch. Leaning against the rail, she stared out at the overgrown cotton fields. She took a long deep breath and felt herself age another year or two. She knew she would have to deal with reality, not lounge around in her daydreams, as her mother so often did. Bitterness welled up again, putting a bad taste in her mouth.

She turned and walked inside the house. In the hall, she spotted her father's Bible on the mahogany table. Something prompted her to reach for it and hug it gently against herself.

She had not read her Bible in a very long time, not since she had been carrying on this personal war with God. Now, she traced her fingers on the leather cover, seeing the chipped places and wishing the Bible could talk back to her. How she longed to know what Father had experienced, where he had been, what had finally happened to him.

Holding the Bible, she walked back outside and sat down in the chair once again. She opened the Bible to the center and began to read Psalms, always her favorite book. She had learned Psalm 23 by heart as a little girl, and she had made her parents proud by reciting it to them. As she read the chapter again, each word seemed to speak to her personally.

She looked up from the Bible and stared blankly across the yard, thinking. If the Lord was her shepherd, truly *her* shepherd, then He was supposed to guide her through the valleys, beside still water, and He was to restore her soul.

Restoring her soul would be a major task, she thought, yet the verses brought pleasant memories of childhood with her family seated together around the hearth. Her parents were deeply religious, and she had always marveled that they could be so trusting of God.

For years, she herself had thought God had forsaken them, yet. . . She felt a wave of tenderness sweep through her. Yet Jonathan had come to them; her earthly father had sent him, or perhaps the heavenly Father had a hand in it as well.

For the first time, a small glimmer of hope began to flicker within her, like a tiny delicate flame sputtering to life. If she nurtured that hope, believed in it, trusted God as her parents always had, maybe He would prepare that table of plenty before them, maybe their cup would run over again. Maybe He would somehow restore their souls.

She turned the page and saw that her father had marked verse five; she looked at it, wondering why. Frowning, she read on.

Thou preparest a. . . He had marked through *table* and written *treasure.* Then the text continued *before me in the. . .* Here he had marked through *presence* and written *New Bethany Church.*

You anoint my. . . He had marked through *head with oil* and written *field with apple trees.*

As Grace read on, she saw that none of the other verses were marked. At the end of the psalm, he had written the words: *October 3, 1863.*

Staring at the date, an odd chill began at the base of her spine and slowly worked its way up her spinal cord and settled in the nerve center at her neck. She reread the passage again. And again.

The door opened behind her, and her mother stepped outside.

"I've peeled the potatoes and covered them with water. They're on the hearth now," she said with a smile.

Grace hadn't heard a word. "Mother, did you see what Father wrote in the Bible he sent to you? Here in Psalm 23? Does this mean anything to you?" She fired the questions at her mother so fast that at first her mother seemed confused.

Looking from Grace to the Bible in her lap, then back at Grace, her mother sat down in the nearest chair.

"Here, Mother. Look at this again."

Grace watched the tiny frown of concentration slip over her mother's forehead as her eyes moved over each verse and then lingered on the inscriptions. She looked up at Grace. "When Jonathan gave me your father's Bible, I read Psalm 23 right away because this psalm was our favorite."

She looked back at the verse. "I didn't understand why Fred had written those words in; then I finally decided he was making a reference to the apple trees we helped plant in the church yard. You remember how he loved apples?"

Grace reached over and gripped her mother's hand.

"Mother, I believe this is a code. Look at the date at the end of the chapter."

"Yes, I saw that too. I assumed that was the last time he read it."

Grace jumped out of the chair and began to pace the porch, her mind jumping from one word to another, and ending up again on the date he had written at the end of the psalm.

"Mother, why would Father be so insistent on Jonathan bringing that Bible all the way back down here to us? He told him to put the Bible in your hands, remember? Why would he ask a stranger, for he was a stranger in some ways, to personally deliver the Bible to us? That doesn't make sense unless he had a very strong motive for. . .as he said, putting the Bible in your hands. He knew you would read that psalm, which had been a favorite of yours and his; and he took a chance that you would understand."

Elizabeth gasped. "Oh, Grace. If you're right, it would have been a terrible thing for me not to interpret his message. But remember the other thing. Fred wanted Jonathan to let us know. . .what had happened to him."

"Yes, but Jonathan also said he kept mentioning the church. Don't you remember? We thought he meant go to any church, or perhaps to the church down the road. But he meant for us to go back to New Bethany Church to look for the treasure under the apple tree. Oh, Mother, it all makes sense now."

Elizabeth nodded and looked at the inscriptions again. "Freddy used to dress up and pretend he was an explorer when he was a little boy. He always had your father send him notes about buried treasure—"

"You see, that's it! I believe with all of my heart Father was sending a message to us. And I intend to go to New Bethany Church and find that treasure, just as he intended us to."

"But a treasure?" her mother asked, reading the verse again.

"I don't know what's buried there, Mother, but if it was important enough for Father to get the message to us, I owe it to him—and to us—to see what he left there."

She looked down the driveway and saw Jonathan walking back toward the house.

"What are you going to do, Grace?" Her mother stood up, looking anxious for the first time.

Grace laced her fingers together, pressing against her palms, and considered the choices she had, which were indeed limited. Her eyes followed the slow easy gait of the man who had come on a mission from her father, a mission that could change their lives.

"If Father trusted Jonathan Parker, then I think we have every right to believe he thought we could trust him as well." As Jonathan grew closer, she whispered her decision to her mother. "I'm going to ask Jonathan to go with me to Sand Mountain. If I'm right and Father hid any kind of treasure there, then I'll offer to share it with Jonathan in return for his help."

A frown worked its way over her mother's forehead. "Grace, we can't be sure about this. And I don't want to risk losing you." She reached out, gripping her hand and looking at her with pleading eyes.

"You aren't going to lose me, Mother," Grace said, hugging her mother and feeling her ribs beneath her fingertips. Her mother had lost more weight. In her father's absence, Grace knew she had to be strong for both of them.

She placed her hands on her mother's shoulders and leaned back to look into her kind hazel eyes. "Your faith has kept you strong and courageous; this morning, I decided that it's time for me to start acting more like you. Please forgive me for doubting your faith," she said, watching the sheen of tears appear in her mother's eyes.

"I love you, Grace," her mother said, looking frail and vulnerable again.

"And I love you. And we're going to be all right, Mother. We will get through these hard times, and we'll be strong again."

"Grace, you've always been strong. Just like Fred."

They were smiling through their tears as Jonathan reached the porch. Looking from one to the other, his face registered surprise.

"Is everything okay?" he asked.

"Everything is just fine," Grace said, smiling at him.

"That's good. Well, I have the gate repaired," he said, looking very pleased about it.

"Thank you so much," Grace said. Her heart was beating faster as she watched him climb the steps and settle into the chair beside her. He had changed into work clothes, and in the faded blue shirt, he was just as handsome as he had been in his nice suit.

"Reams is going to ride over to visit his cousins this afternoon. You remember he mentioned they need work. Maybe he can talk them into coming here and between you and Mr. Douglas, you can come to some kind of agreement with them."

"Thank you." Grace looked at him, wondering for one last time if it were safe to trust him. She was certain that God had sent him to them; after all, he had been the one to bring the Bible with the important message. In her heart, she knew that it was safe to trust this man.

"Come inside," she said to Jonathan, glancing at her mother. "We need to discuss something with you."

Jonathan took a look at her and hesitated. "You sound very serious."

"Yes, please come in so we can talk," she said, automatically glancing around her. She was constantly looking over her shoulder, even though with Jonathan at their side, she felt more safe than she had since the war began.

Once they were in the dining room, seated at the table drinking coffee, Grace opened her father's Bible to Psalm 23. She handed the Bible to Jonathan.

"Read these verses, and notice what my father has marked. Then tell me what you think."

Elizabeth had entered the dining room and sat at the end of the table, watching Jonathan as he read the verses.

Grace watched his eyebrows lift. He stopped reading for a moment and looked at her but said nothing. Then he began reading again. When he had finished, he shook his head.

"In a way, this is pretty confusing to me. It does strike me as odd that he has marked through these verses and made some notations. What seems strangest of all is the date here. October 3, 1863."

"That's exactly what I think."

Jonathan looked over Grace's head to the window, as though pondering something. Then he looked back at Grace. "Your father told me he joined up with General Braxton Bragg when he came through northern Alabama after leaving Shiloh. Your father would have been in the Battle of Chattanooga and Chickamauga in the fall. That's when he wrote this date in the Bible."

"Then he wasn't too far from Sand Mountain at that time," Elizabeth interjected. "Jonathan, we moved down here to Pickens County from Sand Mountain, where we had lived for eleven years. While we lived there, we helped to build New Bethany Church at Pine Grove. Fred and I planted an apple tree in front of the church."

"You see," Grace turned back to Jonathan. "I'm absolutely certain this is a code from my father. I don't understand its full meaning, but I believe with all of my heart that my father left something at New Bethany Church for us. And Jonathan. . ." She paused and took a deep breath, gathering her courage to ask. "I know you need to get back to Kentucky, but I want to make a deal with you."

"A deal?" he asked, looking from Grace to her mother.

She hesitated, wondering for a moment what kind of deal he thought she was going to propose to him. "Yes, a deal." She plunged on. "Obviously I cannot go that distance by myself." She hesitated, glancing at her mother. "Well, if I had no choice, I would probably strike out on my own, in spite of Mother's protests."

"You know I wouldn't allow you to do that," Elizabeth spoke up nervously, her gaze darting from Grace to Jonathan.

"You want me to go with you," Jonathan said, sparing her the discomfort of having to ask.

"Yes, and if Father has hidden a treasure there, I will share it with you for helping me. Whatever it is."

He shook his head. "I wouldn't feel right doing that. Your father saved my life and—"

"And you saved his life before that. Please, Jonathan, tell me you'll go with me. Then after I satisfy myself as to whether or not there is something there, I promise not to ask anything more of you. In fact, we can part company at Sand Mountain, and you can go on to Kentucky."

He shook his head. "I can't allow you to make the trip back alone. But Grace, before you get your hopes up, I have to tell you something. It's quite likely that your father buried money, not knowing for sure that Confederate money would lose its value."

"That's true," Grace sighed. "But even if that's what is buried there, I still will be glad to go and find out for myself."

Jonathan nodded. "I wish we could find someone else to go with you, Grace. Or go for you. I've been out of service for a month now. I really need to go on to Kentucky."

Elizabeth spoke up. "Jonathan, I wonder if you could send a wire to your family, letting them know that you are safe but that you've been detained."

Grace brightened. "Yes! That's a good idea, Mother." She looked at Jonathan. "The telegraph is back in operation in some areas. Surely along the way. . ."

He raked his fingers through his dark hair as though wrestling with his decision. For a moment, Grace had a terrible feeling that he was going to say no, but then as he looked back at her mother, he slowly began to smile.

"All right. I'll wire my brother-in-law at the first place we come to." He heaved a deep sigh. "Grace, we'll go to this New Bethany Church and see if you're right about this. If your father buried something there, we'll do our best to find it."

"Maybe he buried gold," Elizabeth said quietly.

"But where would he get gold? That's the only part that bothers me," Grace said, trying to figure it all out. "I believe he did send us this message, and I think it all makes sense. But where would he get gold, or even enough money to consider a treasure, for that matter? He was fighting in a war."

"An officer gave me a horse," Jonathan countered, looking from Grace to her mother. "Maybe someone paid your father for saving a life or just for helping. Or did he have something he could have sold?"

Again, Grace looked to her mother for answers.

"He had his gold watch, which wouldn't be that valuable," she said. "I honestly don't know. But I believe this is a message from God." Grace's mother folded her hands together and smiled. "God began to answer our prayers when you came to us with news from Fred, Jonathan. And I believe those answers are just beginning."

She took a deep breath. "Grace, after thinking about it, I would like to ask Jonathan to go without you. That's a long trip, and it would be too hard on you."

"No, Mother." Grace frowned. "I want to go; I have to go."

"But Grace. . ." Elizabeth looked from Grace to Jonathan. "I hesitate to mention this, but we must consider how it will look to other people, the two of you traveling alone."

Jonathan looked at her mother, understanding her meaning, then back at Grace. "She's right. I can make the trip alone."

"No." Grace stood up. "Mother, this is no time to be worrying about what other people think. I'm going, and there's no talking me out of it."

Jonathan grinned at her. "I can see there's no point in trying. Mrs. Cunningham, I think I need to assure you that I will take very good care of Grace. I will not say or do anything to reflect badly on her. Or upon me," he added.

Grace felt her cheeks flush as she darted a glance at her mother. They were all talking about the same thing: if Jonathan could be trusted not to take advantage of her on this long trip.

"I believe you," Elizabeth said, "and I don't want to offend you."

He smiled and touched her hand. "You are just being a good mother, and I certainly respect that. I promise you," he said, looking into her eyes, "that I will behave as a gentleman at all times."

"That settles it then," Grace said, wanting to get on with planning the trip. "Jonathan, while we're making deals here, you must agree to accept half of whatever we find."

"Grace is right," Elizabeth said. "You must accept half of whatever you two find there. We have always dealt fairly with people, and to ask anything more of you would be completely unfair."

Grace looked at Jonathan. She could see the inner battle he was waging. But then he began to shake his head slowly, and he put his hands out, palms up.

"How can I refuse two charming, persuasive ladies? Grace, can you be ready to travel at daylight?"

"I'm ready now," she answered eagerly.

He chuckled. "I'm sure you are, but we need to make some plans. I have some maps in my saddlebag, and I want to study the terrain. Also, we need to get the horses ready and. . ." His voice trailed. "I forgot you only have the gray horse."

"Molly will take me wherever I need to go," Grace said, feeling totally confident in Molly's ability.

"Are you sure?" He was obviously not as confident.

"Yes, I am. But if Molly quits on me, I can always ride behind you, can't I?"

"Well, yes. But—"

"Or if we do find gold, I can buy another horse. You see, I have it all figured out."

"I believe you do. It's settled then. We'll go. Mrs. Cunningham, how long will it take us to reach the area where you lived?"

Elizabeth pursed her lips. "We came in a wagon with extra horses, and it took us four days."

"So you camped three nights on the road," Jonathan said, glancing worriedly at Grace.

"Yes, but one night we stayed with some friends along the way who had been neighbors at Sand Mountain. And that reminds me, Grace, you know the Copeland family up around Jasper. You could stay one night at Ethel Copeland's house. Ethel would be pleased to have you. She's a very nice person."

Grace nodded. Ethel Copeland was a sister to Mrs. Douglas, and she and her husband had visited at Oak Grove during the summer and again at Christmas every year before the war began.

"Yes, I think we would be welcome at Mrs. Copeland's house. But I don't know if I can find her place."

"Just stop somewhere in Jasper and ask. Everyone knows Ethel Copeland. Her husband worked at the bank until he died."

Jonathan was deep in thought as they discussed the Copelands, but at the first opportunity he spoke up again. "We need to think about the route we'll take to get to Sand Mountain, Grace. I came down from Chattanooga through Huntsville, but it took three days of hard riding."

His blue eyes were filled with concern as he faced Grace. "Are you sure you're up to that kind of travel?" He began to smile for she had already begun to roll her eyes. "On second thought, I guess you can do about anything you put your mind to, am I right?"

"You are exactly right." She grinned at him.

"You'll need to take food," Elizabeth said, getting out of her chair to go into the kitchen to check the shelves in the pantry.

Jonathan and Grace got up to follow.

"I traveled with dried beans and salt pork in my saddle bag," Jonathan said. "There's still a small ration there. I keep a couple of cooking pans with me as well. Of course, we can stop at a store along the way and pick up rations as we need them."

"We have plenty of biscuits in the kitchen," Grace said, recalling how much he had enjoyed her biscuits.

"And I'll make up some corn dodgers," her mother called from inside the pantry.

Jonathan was puzzled. "Corn dodgers?"

"They're fried corn meal but very tasty," Grace explained. "Not like that mixture you ate with the army."

"I used to prepare them for Fred when he was going to be out for awhile." Elizabeth's head popped around the door of the pantry. "You remember how he loved my corn dodgers, Grace?"

"Yes." Grace was thinking about clothes. "What else do we need, Jonathan?"

"I'll make a list," he said. "And I'll check your saddle and harness to see if they need any patching. I'll refill the canteen." He paused, then looked toward the pantry where they could hear Elizabeth rummaging around. "What about your mother?" he asked, shaping the question with his lips so that Elizabeth wouldn't hear.

Grace turned and looked toward the pantry. Why hadn't she thought of this sooner? She couldn't go off and leave her mother by herself. Then she thought of the usual answer: their neighbors, the Douglases.

"Jonathan, could you ride over to Mr. Douglas's place and see if Reams and his wife could come stay with Mother? I'll send a note saying. . .I'm not sure what I'll say."

"Why don't you let me think of something?" her mother suggested as she stepped out of the pantry. "In fact, don't worry about it now. I'm sure Reams will be over sometime today, and I'll ask him."

Grace nodded in agreement to the plan. "A note from you will be much more convincing, Mother. Mr. Douglas isn't about to say no to you."

They laughed together, and Grace breathed a sigh of relief. It seemed that finally God was beginning to answer their prayers.

eight

They left at first light the next morning. True to his word, Jonathan had both horses ready for travel, and he had stocked saddlebags with rations and drawn out a map for them to follow.

Grace was thankful they were traveling north and would not have to return to Whites Creek. For now, she wanted to put as much distance as possible between them and Sonny.

They set off at a brisk pace and had ridden for over an hour in silence. Grace had promised herself not to be a chatterbox or worry Jonathan unnecessarily. They had agreed to ride faster the first few hours while the horses were fresh, so conversation was scarce as they cantered their horses up the main road.

Only once did Grace worry about their safety. They had rounded a curve and come face-to-face with a man riding toward them on a sway-backed mule. He was the worst looking man Grace had ever seen. Beneath a cap of animal fur, his skin was blackened from smoke; the smell of fire was strong upon him. His clothes were filthy and ragged, and there was a strange glint in his hard eyes. Once they were close to him, he looked away as though avoiding their open stares.

After he was well behind them, Jonathan turned to Grace. "I've seen several men like that along the way. Bummers, they're called. They're thieves who roam the country, stealing, killing. You see now why I'm concerned for you and your mother."

Grace glanced back over her shoulder as the old mule and

the strange man disappeared around the curve. "I think I'm better off not knowing about people like that," she said, wishing that she had never seen the man whose image was sure to haunt her memory, particularly in the middle of the night when she jumped at the slightest sound. "I hope Mother is all right," she said. She had hated to leave her mother for whom she felt so responsible.

"With Reams and his wife there, she'll be safe while we're gone."

Grace nodded. "Yes, thank God for Reams and Chloe."

Every bone in Grace's body ached by the time they reached Jasper, but she would have bitten her tongue off before she complained. They stopped to ask directions to Mrs. Copeland's house once they reached the outskirts of Jasper. As it turned out, they were only a short distance from their destination, and it was a relief to Grace to turn Molly up the circular drive to the brick house.

Grace studied the house, sitting at the top of the hill, recalling the fun she and Freddy had enjoyed when her parents had visited the Copelands. For a moment, her throat felt tight when she recalled those days, but she forced her mind to the task at hand: reminding Mrs. Copeland who she was so they could stay overnight.

Darkness was settling over the front porch as she wearily climbed the steps and knocked on the front door. She could hear footsteps moving quickly, approaching the entrance. Then the door opened, and Mrs. Copeland stood before her, looking as though she knew Grace but couldn't quite place her.

In the two years since Grace had seen the woman, Mrs. Copeland's hair had turned gray. Also, she was much thinner, which was not a surprise to Grace. Almost every woman she saw was thin because of the hardships they had faced during the war.

"Mrs. Copeland, I'm Grace Cunningham. My family lives on the farm adjoining the Douglases in Pickens County. Do you remember me?"

"Of course I do!" Mrs. Copeland responded. "Land's sake, what a beauty you've become. Do come in," she called, looking over Grace's head to Jonathan.

"Mrs. Copeland, this is Jonathan Parker," Grace made the introduction as he removed his hat and bowed. "Before he opens his mouth, I must tell you that he's from Kentucky, but he befriended my father during the war. And now he's doing a great favor for my mother and me, seeing me back to Sand Mountain."

"Hello, Mr. Parker. Come inside, both of you."

After a day spent looking at rough terrain for miles on end, Grace welcomed the feel of the cozy little house, where crocheted doilies, comfortable sofas, and chairs gave a sense of home.

Just then another woman came to the doorway of the kitchen, surveying them curiously.

"This is my older sister, Edith," Mrs. Copeland said. "Edith, come say hello to Grace Cunningham and her friend, Jonathan Parker."

"Cunningham?" Edith repeated, staring at first Grace, then Jonathan.

"Yes, you remember Elizabeth and Fred Cunningham. How are they, Grace?" Mrs. Copeland asked, smiling.

Grace took a deep breath. "Father died last month in Chattanooga," she replied. "And Freddy was killed in battle in '62."

Mrs. Copeland shook her head sadly. "I am so sorry, my dear. My Robert died before the war. And you know we never had any children, so I don't know the agony of losing a son in the war. Your poor mother." She sighed and began to lead them into the kitchen. "Come in."

"Now which Cunningham is this, Ethel?" Edith inquired, looking blank.

Grace glanced at her and decided the woman was well into her sixties and obviously a bit forgetful.

Ethel went into more detail about how she and her husband had been neighbors. Meanwhile Grace looked around the kitchen. A teapot and cups sat on a small table covered with a white cloth.

"We don't want to impose," Jonathan spoke up, when at last he had an opportunity.

"Not at all. We have plenty of room here, with only Edith and me to rattle around in this big house."

They laughed together, then sat down at the table for a meal of meatloaf and potatoes. Grace tried not to eat too much food, but she gave up when Mrs. Copeland brought out an apple pie. After stuffing themselves and chatting for another hour, Jonathan stood.

"If you ladies will excuse me, I'll say goodnight."

"Your room is at the far end of the hall upstairs. Last door on the left."

Jonathan thanked her again and left the women alone to talk about happy times during the summers they had visited. Within the hour, Grace began to nod. Mrs. Copeland showed her to her room, and Grace only had time to admire it briefly before collapsing into bed and sleeping like a baby.

They saddled up and rode out of Jasper early the next morning after saying good-bye to Ethel and Edith. Both knew it would be a long, hard day, so they decided not to waste time and energy with conversation. They rode hard, stopping only for a quick lunch by a stream where they could water their horses and rest the animals for an hour. Then they were on the road again.

By midafternoon, Grace was wondering how much longer she could stay in the saddle. She was not accustomed to such long rides, but she didn't remind Jonathan of that. If he were willing to go to the time and trouble to take her to Sand Mountain, the least she could do was be a good sport and not complain. She had known the trip would be difficult before she'd left home, and she had been determined to go. Yet a deep ache was settling into her bones when she spotted a small community at the next bend in the road.

"Let's stop here and check supplies," Jonathan suggested. "I'll ask someone about the road ahead. I thought we'd camp tonight, if you feel you're up to it."

"Sure." Grace forced a smile, but all she could think about was how comfortable Mrs. Copeland's bed had felt the previous night and that she was already twice as tired as she had been then.

The community turned out to hold no more than basic shops, but they picked up some dried apples, and Jonathan spoke with the man at the livery about the road north where they were traveling.

As they rode out of town, Jonathan promised only another hour of riding before they would stop. This time Grace agreed. "I'll be ready; I don't think I can go much farther."

When Jonathan led the way off the road and through a grassy meadow toward a small stream, Grace heaved a deep sigh of relief and began to feel better. She was pleased to see that Jonathan knew what he was doing when it came to finding a good camping spot for the night. He had chosen a level spot near the small creek. They were about three hundred yards upstream from where the wagon road crossed the creek.

"We'll be safer if we don't camp too near the road," he explained to her as they picketed their horses. "Do you mind dipping a can of water from the stream over there?" he added as he gathered up leaves and pine straw.

"What are you doing?" she asked, looking at the pine straw.

"This will keep the ground from being too hard beneath your quilt," he answered and kept working.

She smiled to herself. He was such a considerate man. The longer she was with him and the better she got to know him, the more she liked Jonathan Parker.

Later, settled down before the fire, they sipped their coffee and enjoyed the feeling of a full stomach for the first time all day. After a meal of dried apples, beans, and salt pork, Grace began to relax. Just sitting beside Jonathan and staring at the low campfire was comforting to her. She was no longer nervous around him or even shy. She felt like she had known him all of her life. It was strange for her to think about him that way, when they had come from such different parts of the country and had been on opposite sides of the war. But none of that really mattered to her now. Jonathan Parker was the kind of man she had always dreamed of meeting, but she had begun to believe that she never would. She stared at the flickering flames of the campfire, still amazed by all that had happened.

"Are you okay?" Jonathan asked.

"Fine." She looked at him, admiring the way the firelight danced over his handsome face and lit his deep blue eyes. "I'm sorry I was so rude to you when you came to our house," she said, suddenly thinking about the first time she ever saw him.

"I didn't expect you to greet me with open arms, certainly not when you heard me speak and realized I was a Yankee."

She reached over to touch his hand. "You are such a kind and tolerant person. You are slow to anger, slow to take offense, and always willing to give people the benefit of the doubt. I really admire you for that, Jonathan."

"And you are quite a woman," he said, squeezing her hand. "You have a beauty that shines from your heart, and I admire you very much. I think you're probably the most courageous woman I've ever met."

She laughed. "Courageous? You mean the way I struck out on this crazy mission to the north of Alabama?"

"Let's hope it isn't crazy. Yes, I admire you for that, but I also respect the way you've taken charge of your situation at home, trying to make the most of a terrible ordeal. And I admire the way you have taken care of yourself and your mother."

"Thank you. Oh, Jonathan," she said, staring into the fire, "I hope Father has something important waiting for us. If so, maybe there's hope of saving the farm and starting over again."

She leaned back and hugged her knees. Her riding habit was wrinkled and soiled at the knee, but she didn't care. She felt so happy sitting beside Jonathan, daring to hope and dream once again. Tilting her head back, she looked up at the stars. It was a black velvet night with a thousand tiny lights twinkling across the heavens.

Jonathan reached over to press a kiss to her cheek. She leaned closer, but he pulled back from her, chuckling softly. She turned and looked at him. "And just why are you laughing, Mr. Parker?"

"I was just reminding myself of my promise to your mother to behave like a gentleman. And that means its time to pitch my bedroll on the opposite side of the campfire."

"Don't get too far from me," she said, glancing at the spot where he had laid his bedroll. She would feel safe with him there.

He stood up, still holding her hand. "Sweet dreams, Grace. I hope they're of me."

She smiled up at him.

Later, as she snuggled down into her quilts and drifted off to sleep, she thought how good it felt to sleep out under the stars. As she listened to Jonathan's steady breathing from the opposite side of the campfire, she hugged her pillow and slept even better than the night before.

❧

The next morning, they left at daybreak with a fierce determination to make it as far as they could. At noon, with the sun high in the sky, they stopped beside a stream to water and graze their horses and to rest and snack on a light lunch.

"You've been a good companion on this trip," Jonathan said, as they dropped down on a grassy spot under the wide branches of a leafy oak. "You haven't complained about sleeping on the hard ground or riding for miles on end without stopping. I feel certain if I were with my sisters, I would have heard a lot of complaints long before now. But then, neither of my sisters would have the backbone to make this kind of trip. On second thought, Katherine might do it, now that she's older."

He took a bite of biscuit and smiled at her. "And nobody can make biscuits like this. Not even my mother."

"Thank you, Sir. I've been told that anytime a man tells you that you can do something *almost* as good as his mother, it's a genuine compliment. But you've taken that compliment even further. I promise never to tell your mother, though."

They looked at each other, and she shook her head. "What am I saying? Unfortunately, I'll never get to meet your mother."

His eyes ran over her features, and he winked at her. "Don't be too sure about that. You never know what the future will bring."

She arched an eyebrow. "I don't think the future will bring me to Louisville."

"But you can't be sure," he said, grinning. Then he got up to check on the horses. As her eyes followed him, Grace wondered why he had said that to her. How she longed to know what he really thought of her. How tempted she was to simply ask him.

She had always prided herself on being independent, but

she could feel that independence slipping. She liked to be with Jonathan so much that even now she felt a bit lonesome when he wandered off with the horses to explore the road ahead. She turned and reached for another biscuit. As she took a bite, she smiled to herself.

Maybe if they found a valuable buried treasure, she could buy her way into his heart and persuade him to stay at Riverwood. If he wanted to raise horses, he could do that very easily at their farm. And she might as well go on and tell him that she couldn't think of anything in the world she would rather do than work with horses.

She smiled to herself, feeling very good about the idea.

☙

When they were back on the trail again, Grace asked, "How much longer do you think it will take us?"

"The best I can calculate is late afternoon. I found the community of Pine Grove on my map. From the directions your mother gave me, the church should only be a mile or so east of there on the main road."

She smiled, wondering exactly what awaited them at the church.

They rode along in silence that was broken occasionally when Jonathan talked about his childhood or told funny stories that he had heard over the years. Grace laughed with him. She thought about how compatible they were and said as much to him.

"I know," he nodded, looking at her. "I've thought how nice it would have been if only we had met in another time, another place."

She looked at the pine thicket across the road. She didn't want to think about what those words meant because they had a tragic sound to them. It was the kind of thing one would admit before you said good-bye. She blinked and looked back at the road.

Once they found the treasure, everything would change. She would be able to convince him that he belonged with her in Alabama. Yes, once they had money, everything would be all right.

They reached Pine Grove sooner than they had hoped. It was only two o'clock in the afternoon when they turned their horses down the narrow street that led through the small community.

"Do you want to stop here?" he asked.

"No, let's keep going," she said, glancing around.

As in all small communities, the few people out on the sidewalks were staring at them as they rode past. It was a relief once they were on the outskirts of Pine Grove headed in the direction of the church.

In less than an hour, they spotted the white clapboard church with its little steeple at the crest of a hill. They glanced at each other and kneed their horses to move faster toward the little building nestled in a grove of pine and oak trees. At the corner of the churchyard, Grace could see an apple tree.

Her heart beat faster as their horses climbed the hill to the church.

"It looks lonely and forlorn, don't you think?" Grace asked in a hushed voice.

"Yes. But why are you whispering?"

She glanced at him and saw the humor in his face. She laughed. "Well, I was always taught to be respectful around God's house."

She gazed up at the little steeple, a beacon to those who needed a place to worship.

"I haven't been to church in over two years," Grace said, feeling a bit guilty as they approached the small churchyard. She wasn't sure why she felt compelled to say that, but she did. She only hoped God would believe how truly sorry she was for the mean things she had said about Him.

"Well, let's start praying that we find what your father intended us to find beneath that tree," Jonathan said, taking a deep breath.

Glancing at him, she realized that he too was nervous. She was so excited that she could hardly stay in the saddle. She wanted to bolt down from the horse and run the rest of the way.

"Mother talked about when they came to dinners on the ground here," she said, realizing she had to talk to vent her nervousness, or else she would start screaming.

"Dinners on the ground?"

"This was before they had tables in the churchyards. Everyone brought food, and the women spread quilts over the ground like a giant tablecloth for the food."

"What about ants?"

"They just added flavor."

They reached the edge of the churchyard, and Jonathan got down from his horse and looked around. Grace scrambled off Molly before he could help her down. She couldn't wait another minute to get to that apple tree.

"The last words your father spoke before I left were about the church," Jonathan said, as he tied General to a low limb while Grace tied Molly.

"Tell me what he said one more time," Grace instructed, wishing she could have seen her father before he died.

"He said, 'Go to the church.'" Jonathan reached for Grace's hand as they began to walk toward the apple tree. "It begins to make sense now."

"I hope so." Grace replied, walking stiff-legged toward the tree. She no longer felt the ache of so many hours in the saddle, or the dull headache.

They had reached the apple tree where heavy weeds and thick grass covered the ground. Grace dropped to her knees, crawling around in the grass. Her fingers combed through the thick tufts of grass, searching for an area that might indicate a hiding place. Jonathan dropped down beside her, and together they covered every inch of ground around the apple tree. Neither spoke a word.

Slowly Grace sat back on her heels, looking all around them. Had she been mistaken? Had she just wished so hard for a miracle that she had tried to create one?

She looked across at Jonathan, who heaved a weary sigh and sat down in the grass.

"I–I'm sorry," she said, trying desperately not to cry. She couldn't bear the disappointment she felt creeping through her, ready to settle into her heart and send her hopes plummeting once again.

He reached over and squeezed her hand. "So am I." He looked back at the sturdy little tree. "I checked the area right at the base of the tree. I don't think its possible that anything has been buried here."

Grace's throat ached as fiercely as her head, and she pulled up her knees to rest her head. She couldn't bear to think of the time they had wasted or the trouble she had caused Jonathan.

"Maybe there's another apple tree around somewhere."

Her head shot up, and she winced in pain at the sudden movement. She looked all around the front of the church, but there was no other apple tree.

"Come on, let's search the entire area." He stood and extended his hand, helping her up. "We're not giving up yet."

They circled around the church to the back where the grass was knee-high. Thirty feet further, a small iron fence enclosed eight graves.

"A cemetery," Grace said, frowning at Jonathan as they walked in that direction.

The rusty old gate creaked when Jonathan pushed it open, and they entered the cemetery. Grace glanced at the tombstones. All the names were the same.

"One entire family is buried here," she said softly.

"Probably died of typhoid because all the deaths are in the same year except for one."

Grace looked at the small grave and imagined a baby had been stillborn.

"Grace, look!" Jonathan pointed toward the back of the cemetery, which was overgrown with brambles and bushes. In the very back corner, Grace spotted a small tree.

Her eyes met Jonathan's, and he grabbed her hand as they walked carefully around the grave sites until they reached the remote little tree.

An apple tree.

Grace caught her breath and squeezed Jonathan's hand. Again, her hopes were soaring. *God, please,* she silently prayed.

At the base of the tree, there appeared to be a small grave, even though weeds had sprouted over some of the bare spots. A large flat rock served as a tombstone, and on the rock was written the word Cunningham.

"Wait a minute," Jonathan frowned. "It's Cunningham. Grace, did your parents lose a baby?"

"I don't think so. Freddy was the first child. I know that because I've heard Mother talk about how much trouble she'd had giving birth to Freddy since he was the first one. He was only four years older than I. I'm certain no child was born between Freddy and me. At least I think I'm certain."

"Maybe you were too young to remember; maybe they just never told you about another baby; the baby could have been stillborn."

Grace stared at the rock, and her heart began to beat faster.

"No, Jonathan. Father would have had a proper tombstone for one of his children. He would never use a rock on the grave. And look—even the name is crudely written."

Jonathan nodded, dropping down beside the flat rock. It

was about twelve inches wide, and about twenty inches high, roughly inscribed with the initial *F. Cunningham, 1863*.

Jonathan examined the ground underneath the rock, where no grass had grown. In the soft moist earth lay a tiny piece of something that glimmered beneath its coat of dirt. Jonathan dusted it off and held it up.

The late afternoon sunlight drifted down through the little branches of the apple tree and touched the object, which shone pure gold. "A gold coin," Jonathan said, smiling at Grace.

"Oh, Jonathan. Maybe. . ." But she could say no more, for she was suddenly too nervous to speak.

"I'll get the shovel," he said, hurrying off.

Grace cast a furtive glance around the woods, then the cemetery, as she sat clutching the coin against her heart. *God, please.*

Those two words had become a litany for her that she couldn't seem to finish because she didn't know how to ask for gold. All she could whisper were those two words: *God, please.*

nine

"I think I've found something," Jonathan said after shoveling out about twelve inches. "It's leather, may be a saddlebag. Yes, that's what it is!"

He carefully dug out more dirt, exposing a dark brown, almost black, leather saddlebag, badly molded and showing sign of rot and deterioration.

The leather strap he pulled on broke, so he dug out some more dirt, uncovering the full side of the upper bag. As he lifted the bag, he said, "It sure is heavy."

Grace looked right and left, her heart racing. She couldn't see a soul anywhere, nor could she hear anyone. "Is there anything else?" she whispered.

Jonathan reached down into the hole, testing the ground around it with the shovel. "I don't think so. I think this is what your father intended for us to find." He stopped digging and dropped the shovel.

"What are you going to do?" she asked, staring at him.

"Let's walk a little deeper into the woods where we're completely out of sight."

Holding the saddlebag against him, he reached for Grace's hand. They stepped through an underbrush of weeds and briars as they hurried to the edge of the woods. Grace glanced back over her shoulder when they stopped underneath an old oak.

Behind them lay the lonely little cemetery with its eight graves that contained a family. She could barely make out the dark outline of the fence and the little church, which seemed a soft white against the graying light.

Jonathan knelt down with the saddlebag. "Say your prayers," he said to her.

"I already have. A hundred times."

He untied the leather straps of the saddlebag, lifted the flap, and reached inside. He pulled out a leather bag with drawstrings pulled tight. Grace pressed against him, straining to see what was inside.

In the gray light, gold coins gleamed. Grace gasped, then covered her mouth with trembling fingers.

"There are a lot of coins," Jonathan whispered. He began to check the offside bag. "Grace, this one is full too."

She still had her fingers clamped over her mouth, afraid to open her lips, not trusting herself to refrain from shouting with joy.

"Clear off a spot on the ground somewhere so we can count them," he said, glancing toward the base of the oak.

Grace scrambled back against the tree and began furiously yanking up weeds and shoving pebbles aside until she had cleared a small area where none of the coins could get lost in weeds or grass.

Jonathan moved back beside her and carefully emptied the bags. Together they began to count the coins. Grace stacked her coins in little piles of twenty. Jonathan methodically counted his. When they totaled up the amount, there was six hundred dollars.

They merely stared at one another for one unbelievable moment. "Quick, put them back," Jonathan said, opening the leather pouch. "Let's count the other one."

An even better surprise awaited them with the next pile of coins.

"There are 720 in this one," Jonathan said, shaking his head in disbelief.

Grace was beyond speaking. Never in her wildest imagination would she have believed that her father had managed to bury this much money and get a message to her. Then, with the help of God, she and Jonathan had found the gold that would change their lives. Yet, she was almost numb with shock. She couldn't even speak. All she could do was close her eyes and say, *Thank you, God.*

When she opened her eyes, she saw that Jonathan was praying too. As they stood, Jonathan unbuttoned his shirt and stuffed the saddlebag against his chest. The bag was so heavy that his shirt gaped open a bit, but it was almost dark, and Grace realized it was smarter to look like two people walking the cemetery hand in hand, than two people with one carrying a saddlebag.

They moved quietly, reverently, past the graves. Although Jonathan was careful to open the gate slowly, the creak seemed to echo through the night, louder than before. Somewhere in the distance something scampered through the woods. Grace began to tremble.

"Just walk fast to the horses, mount up, and we're going to ride off in a normal fashion," Jonathan whispered.

She nodded, her teeth chattering as they marched back to the horses. A light wind whipped through the trees and cooled her skin, but she knew it was not the cool night air that made her weak-kneed. The initial shock had worn off, and she felt as though every nerve in her body was doing a crazy dance beneath her skin.

Once they reached the horses, Jonathan carefully tied the saddlebags in front of the saddle horn, then draped a blanket from his bedroll over the bags.

"I think the smartest thing to do is ride back to Pine Grove. I saw a boardinghouse on the edge of town. We'll have to stay there tonight and leave first thing in the morning."

Grace nodded. She was so grateful to have Jonathan with her to make the decisions. In spite of all her bragging about how she didn't need a man to take care of her, she knew that having the right man beside her made all the difference in the world to her.

All the way back to Pine Grove, Grace kept glancing at Jonathan, thinking he had become as important to her as the gold could ever be. Her wish had come true. Now that she had the gold, she felt certain it would solve her financial problems. Now that she had the gold, she could keep Jonathan. Everything was going to work out just fine.

When they reached the boardinghouse, most of the town had already bedded down for the night. Only a few lanterns still glowed in the windows. Grace could not imagine closing her eyes and sleeping even an hour; she was far too excited.

They pulled into the hitching rail before the frame house with the small sign ROOMS FOR RENT in the window.

"Jonathan, I think I should do the talking," she whispered.

He nodded, and Grace imagined he too was recalling the unpleasant encounter back in Whites Creek.

Jonathan was careful to keep the saddlebag under the folded blanket as they walked up and knocked on the door.

An older man opened the door.

"Good evening," Grace said, smiling at him. "My brother and I are traveling and need rooms for the night. Do you have any?"

The man thrust a lantern in their faces, looking at Grace, then at Jonathan. "Come in."

He stepped aside and opened the door wide. "I'm Wallace Toney. Wife's got some soup on the stove if you're hungry."

"That would be nice," Grace said, glancing at Jonathan as he nodded politely to the man.

"First, I'll show you your rooms." He led them up some rickety steps to the second floor where half a dozen doors were closed. "You can have the first two. Me and the Mrs. Toney have the last one. Those in the middle are occupied by a schoolteacher and a cowboy."

Grace noticed that Jonathan's eyes lingered on the one Mr. Toney had indicated belonging to a cowboy.

"We'll be just fine. Thank you, Mr. Toney."

Jonathan nodded again and headed for the second door as Grace turned in the first one. She stepped inside and closed the door. Once Mr. Toney's footsteps sounded on the stairs, she opened the door again and crept down the hall to knock on Jonathan's door.

He cracked it, then opened it wider as soon as he saw it was Grace.

"I'm not leaving the room," he whispered.

"Good idea. I'll say you aren't feeling well, and I'll bring some soup up to you." She hesitated. "Could you advance me some money to pay for our rooms?"

He reached into his pocket and withdrew two crumpled bills. Grace had the distinct feeling that these might be his last ones.

"I'll be back in a minute," she whispered, slipping the bills into her pocket as she hurried down the stairs.

She followed the aroma of food down the hall to the back of the house and turned into the kitchen. She came up short in the doorway. Seated at the table was a very proper-looking, middle-aged woman, probably the schoolmarm. Opposite her sat a tall, burly looking man with narrow dark eyes who stared lewdly at Grace. The cowboy, she decided, turning toward the stove, where a portly little woman dipped up soup into the serving bowls Mr. Toney was holding.

Grace hurried over to the stove. "My brother is not feeling well, and I'm tired too. If you don't mind, I think I'll take our food upstairs."

Mrs. Toney turned a pleasant round face to her and smiled. "Sure, Honey. That will be just fine. Wallace, get the spoons, why don't you?"

Even with her back turned, Grace felt the man at the table

watching her carefully. She dared not look around. Neither he nor the woman at the table spoke a word to one another.

It seemed to take forever for Mrs. Toney to fill the soup bowls and put them on a tray, along with a napkin and spoons. "Oh, what do you want to drink, Honey?"

"Just water will be fine," Grace said, smiling at her.

Another eternity seemed to pass before her tray held the necessary items. "Thank you very much," she said.

She turned and hurried from the room, back up the stairs, and knocked again on Jonathan's door. "It's me," she whispered.

The door opened three inches as Jonathan peered out to make sure. Then as soon as he opened it wide enough, Grace darted inside, and he closed the door again and turned the key in the lock. She hurried across the room and placed the tray on a bedside table, then sank into the chair beside it.

"The schoolteacher looks unfriendly, and the so-called cowboy looks more like a thief. I don't like his looks one bit, Jonathan."

Jonathan was looking toward the door. "Well, we'll be safe enough here. I've already put Fred's bag away," he finished, grinning at Grace.

"That's good. Fred is very particular about that bag."

Then suddenly they began to laugh, and soon they were laughing so hard they had to cover their mouths to keep from being heard downstairs. They kept on laughing until Grace was holding her stomach and Jonathan was bent double on the floor. When finally their laughter had subsided and Grace was wiping tears from her eyes, Jonathan spoke up.

"I guess we needed a good laugh."

"I guess we did," Grace said with a long sigh.

She heard footsteps up the stairs, then the steps ended at her door. Her eyes shot to Jonathan when she heard a faint knock.

Jonathan crept to the door, slowly turned the key in the

lock, and cracked it. "It's Mr. Toney," he whispered to Grace.

She nodded and hurried past him and out the door. Mr. Toney's eyebrow lifted in shock when she stepped out of Jonathan's room.

"I was getting some money from my brother," she said. "How much do we owe you for our rooms?"

He looked a bit relieved, although Grace wasn't sure he believed the part about Jonathan being her brother.

"A dollar per room," he answered.

Grace thought that was too much, but she was in no position to argue. She withdrew the bills, paid him, and turned toward her door. "Thank you. We'll be leaving first thing."

Once inside the door, she turned the key in the lock. Then she hesitated. She recalled the dark narrow eyes of the man Mr. Toney had described as a cowboy but who looked more like an outlaw. Reaching for a chair, she pushed it against the door and stepped back to be sure it was secure. If the so-called cowboy tried to break through her locked door, he would make enough noise to alert the entire household.

She removed her riding habit and crawled under the covers in her underclothes. Although she managed to get a few hours of sleep, most of the night, she lay in the darkness and stared at the ceiling, wondering how best to use the gold.

Just after daylight, she heard a soft knock on her door. She bolted up in bed and stumbled across the room, listening.

The knocking continued, soft and gentle, then she heard Jonathan call her name softly.

"Yes?" she called to him, reminding herself she was still in her underclothes.

"I'm going to get the horses," he said. "Meet me out front."

"I'll be right there," she called back.

In spite of her fears about the man at the table who lurked in her nightmares during the night, they left Pine Grove without incident. The little community was still asleep, as it had been the night before. They walked their horses out of town, heading south again.

As the day broke, the sun shone brightly, pouring liquid gold over the treetops and lush grass in the meadows. The sweetness of honeysuckle filled the country. Grace rode along, breathing the clean country air, and ventured a glance at Jonathan.

He seemed to be deep in thought as he silently rode on General. She longed to know what he was thinking, but she reminded herself he had a right to his own thoughts without her prying. As though he knew she wondered, he turned to her, looking very serious.

"If you're up to it, I think we should press on as far as we can. We can pay for hotel rooms with gold, and we would be wise to do that. A nice hotel is a good investment in our safety."

"I agree," she said, nodding.

They picked up the pace and didn't bother with conversation as they headed toward their destination for the night.

To Grace's immense relief, the trip passed uneventfully. She had begun the journey back a bundle of nerves. All she could think about, of course, was the gold in the saddlebags. Jonathan was very careful with it at all times, however, so she began to relax by the time they finally pulled into a small town for the night. The strain of nerves and the long trip had worn on both of them, and they kept conversation to a minimum.

They ate their meals, went to their rooms, got up, and left at daybreak each day. On the third day, they rode into Tuscaloosa. More than anything in the world, Grace longed to soak in a tub of hot water with scented soap.

She got her wish when Jonathan obtained rooms for them at the Bradford. It was by far the nicest place they had stayed at during their trip, and Grace asked to have tea and a sandwich sent to her room along with a tub of water. When finally she crawled beneath the clean linen sheets, she closed her eyes and sighed deeply. Then she said what she vowed never to forget again. "Thank You, God."

ten

Over breakfast at the hotel, Jonathan and Grace made their plans. The desk clerk had supplied her with a pen and paper to make the list, and her mind was working furiously.

"Grace, I was thinking we should talk to Mr. Douglas about helping you find some field hands," Jonathan said. "I know we can count on Reams to get us a couple of hands, but you'll need more."

Grace nodded. "Yes, I'll talk to Mr. Douglas."

At the adjoining table in the dining room, an older man and his wife were having breakfast. His accent was not that of a southerner, and Grace had glanced his way as he and his wife discussed plans for their new farm.

Finally, Jonathan turned in his chair and looked at the gentleman. "Excuse me, Sir. I couldn't help overhearing your conversation. We're in town to buy supplies for her farm," he explained, as Grace turned to smile at the couple.

Jonathan stood and extended his hand. "I'm Jonathan Parker, and this is Grace Cunningham."

"How do you do," the man shook his hand. "I'm Bob Templeton, and this is my wife, Barbara."

Grace spoke to her, and they sat back down.

"We just bought a thousand-acre place right outside of Gordo," Mr. Templeton said, looking at Jonathan.

"Yes, Sir. And do you plan to grow cotton?"

"I certainly do. The world is demanding cotton," he said, quite emphatically. "The war reduced cotton production, and now farmers can't supply it fast enough to meet the demand."

"Where did you find your workers?" Jonathan asked with interest.

"Well, for this year, I hired hands just for the season. There are plenty of freed blacks looking for work, but they expect to be paid fairly."

"Of course," Jonathan agreed. "Miss Cunningham expects to do that." He looked back at Grace.

"Oh yes," she agreed.

"Yesterday, I found three Irishmen down at the docks who were looking for work. They're packing up to come to Gordo next week." He paused to drain his coffee cup. "Finding men to work the land isn't a problem if you're willing to pay the price."

"Yes, Sir, I understand," Jonathan said.

The couple stood up, preparing to leave. "It was nice meeting you," the woman said to Grace.

"Thank you. And you too." She looked at the man. "I wish you good luck with your place at Gordo."

Grace watched the couple leave the dining room and wondered what their life would be like. She turned back to Jonathan. "No one is being rude to this man because he speaks. . ." She hesitated, wondering if he would take offense.

"Because he doesn't speak southern," Jonathan supplied, grinning.

"Yes. Oh, Jonathan, maybe in some areas people are beginning to breach the gap between North and South. We mustn't believe that everyone is as terrible as Sonny."

Jonathan shrugged. "I realize that, but remember this man is obviously a man with money, and money talks. It doesn't seem fair to think of it that way, but it's true."

Grace touched his sleeve. "Well, we're prepared to do a bit of talking ourselves, Jonathan. Remember half of what we found belongs to you."

He looked at her and shook his head. "Grace, I don't feel right to take it. You need it more than I do."

"But you will take it. Otherwise, I have been dishonest in my dealings with you, and that isn't right. We made a bargain, and I expect to keep it. Now, what do I need to buy with my half of the money?"

"I will check at the livery and buy two horses and two full sets of harness. Also, I'll find out where I can buy a two-horse wagon. You can go to the store and buy some house supplies and whatever you need. You'll need another hammer, an ax, at least four hoes, and pounds each of ten-penny and twenty-penny nails. I expect you'll want to have some work done on the buildings."

"And the house needs repairs," she added, thinking of what had to be done. For the first time, she could let her mind wander and not feel a whiplash of worry about how she would pay for it. The gold still seemed too good to be true, and she felt like pinching herself several times a day to be sure she was awake, not just dreaming.

"I'll buy some coffee and sugar; we've been out of sugar for more than two years. The first bunch of soldiers took our last sack of sugar. I'll get some salt and pepper and some spices too. I hope to find some pretty cloth for Mother so she can make herself a new dress."

"You should buy yourself some pretty clothes. And some shoes for both of you."

She reached over to squeeze his hand. "You've been so kind and helpful. I could never thank you enough."

"You already have," he answered.

They sat staring into each other's eyes. Again, Grace was certain that Jonathan would stay at Riverwood. She had even allowed herself to dream that they might marry.

"Grace," Jonathan said seriously. "I have to say something to you now. Your father risked his life so that you and your mother could get a start with your land again. None of this belonged to me. I'm more than happy to help you and your mother. What I suggest is that you keep all the money except for two hundred dollars. That will get me back to Kentucky. I don't know what kind of situation I will find when I get there, but I will be two hundred dollars richer than I expected to be."

Grace stared at him, unwilling to believe that he would really leave. How could she persuade him to stay? What could she say? She dropped her gaze to her coffee cup, hoping he wouldn't see the disappointment in her eyes and think it was over the money.

"We'll discuss this later," she said softly.

"We can, but there's no way I will accept more than what I've offered. So, shall we be on our way?"

She looked up and nodded, forcing a smile. As her gaze met his, she wondered if the thought of saying good-bye was as painful to him as to her. There was something in the depths of his blue eyes that had not been there before. As she looked at him, she chose to believe it was sadness at the thought of leaving her.

Squaring her shoulders as they left the dining room, she decided not to accept what he had said as the last word. Somehow she would convince him to stay at Riverwood and help her.

They had decided to stay another day in Tuscaloosa to obtain most of the supplies she would need. For smaller items, she could always go into Whites Creek, but the thought of returning there did not appeal to her.

When Grace and Jonathan finally finished their shopping, she soared with joy and pride. Not only was she riding in a comfortable new wagon, but Jonathan had found her a sorrel mare, four years old. She was fourteen and a half hands high with a white blaze on her forehead and one white stocking on her right front leg. Grace named the mare Lucky for many reasons. Her father had lucked into the gold, buried it, and sent Jonathan into their lives with the good news. Even though she named her horse Lucky, Grace knew the real source of her blessings was God.

The other horse already had the name Banjo, in honor of its former owner. It was fifteen hands high, but together Banjo and Lucky made a matched pair. When Grace bought the horses and knew they were her own, she almost burst into tears. All her life she had wanted a good horse, and now she had two.

Grace and Jonathan stopped in at the livery before leaving town to speak with the owner, Marcus Sawyers. Earlier he had told Jonathan news he had heard about high water from a week's heavy rain in northwest Alabama and Mississippi. The Sipsey and the Tombigbee Rivers had both flooded. Jonathan wanted to get the latest report before they left Tuscaloosa.

Mr. Sawyers shook his head when Jonathan inquired if he had heard any more news of the Sipsey from travelers stopping by.

"For sure. Some folks here last night said the Sipsey River was all out of its banks and in places looked to be a mile wide. How high the Tombigbee is will determine how fast the Sipsey recedes. Sipsey flows into the Tombigbee, you know; so if the Tombigbee gets high, it backs up the Sipsey. Could take a long time for the big river to get back within its banks—as much as a month."

"Oh, no!" Grace gasped, looking at Jonathan.

"May not take that long," Mr. Sawyers said, noticing her concern. "What you'd better do is get back on the other side of the Warrior here so you can hit that wagon road going west. It's a well-traveled road that should be safe, and you can follow it for about six or eight miles, then you'll fork off to the left. That'll keep you on high ground. That road will take you to the ferry where you can cross the Sipsey River. But it may be a day or two wait even there; maybe not."

Jonathan looked at Grace. "That sounds like a good idea. What do you think?"

She nodded in agreement. "If you and Mr. Sawyers think that's best."

"Once you get off the ferry and travel that main road, you'll connect to the main road that you left going through Fayette County on your trip north."

Grace was disappointed to face yet another delay in getting home, but she knew she had to be sensible.

Jonathan thought for a minute. "We'd better go back to the general store and buy some more food, in case we have to wait for the ferry for a few days."

"I suppose so," Grace said as Jonathan turned the wagon around.

"Thanks for the information, Mr. Sawyers," Jonathan called as they rode off.

The news from Mr. Sawyers was the beginning of a bad turn of events for Grace. She found herself sinking into a darker mood for the first time since she and Jonathan had found the gold.

As they turned into the general store, Grace spotted a familiar face, and her heart gave a leap of joy.

"Mrs. Barton," Grace called, waving to the woman who lived near Whites Creek with her husband and family.

Mrs. Barton, dressed in a nice calico with matching sunbonnet turned and looked over her shoulder. Upon seeing Grace, she began to smile and hurry toward the wagon.

"Grace, how nice to see you!"

Grace was already getting down from the wagon to hug Mrs. Barton. She was one of the kindest people Grace had ever known, and she felt certain her kindness would extend to Jonathan.

"Oh, Mrs. Barton. I can't tell you how happy I am to see you. Is Mr. Barton with you?"

Grace liked Mr. Barton as well, and since both were friends of her parents and had often visited in previous years, she began to feel a deep sense of relief sweeping over her.

"Yes, Walter Ray is down at the feed store now. We're here to buy supplies and try and restock some items for the farm."

"So are we!" Grace noticed that Mrs. Barton was looking past Grace to Jonathan, who had reached her side.

Grace made the introductions, explaining who Jonathan was and exactly why he had come to visit them. She hesitated when she got to the part about her father's message, quickly deciding not to mention it or the business with the gold.

"So he graciously agreed to bring me here for shopping."

"How nice," Mrs. Barton replied, shaking his hand. Unlike some others, Mrs. Barton was appreciative of what Jonathan had done, and she said as much to him. "We'll find Walter Ray. Of course, he'll want to see both of you. In fact, why don't you join us for dinner at the hotel?"

Jonathan hesitated, looking at Grace.

"Actually, we just stopped to buy more food here. We were on our way back to Riverwood when we heard about the river. The man at the livery suggested we take a different route."

Mrs. Barton nodded in agreement. "That's right. I heard about the river. You see, we've been here for over a week, and I'm in no hurry to leave," she said, smiling at Grace, then turned back to Jonathan. "If you wish to consider staying on, we would be pleased to have you as part of our group. In fact, we're planning to visit some relatives just out of Tuscaloosa tomorrow. They have a large home and would welcome both of you."

She had been looking from Jonathan to Grace as she spoke. Now she reached forward to squeeze Grace's hand. "Why don't you stay on a few more days? If your mother is all right, then we could travel back to Whites Creek together." She looked at Jonathan. "My husband believes there is safety in numbers."

Jonathan was nodding. "I agree. Grace, this might be the perfect solution. If the Bartons could see you safely back to Riverwood, then I could cut a day off my trip back to Louisville."

The words were like a blow to Grace, and for a moment she thought she was going to reel back into the dirt of the street. For once in her life she was absolutely speechless.

"Oh, you're planning to go back soon?" Mrs. Barton asked, sparing Grace the embarrassment of trying to make conversation.

"Yes. I have a farm in Louisville, and I'm very worried about its condition."

"Are your parents there now?" Mrs. Barton asked with interest.

Grace was conscious of the creak of wagons, the smell of leather, and the *clomp-clomp* of horses around them, but everything else seemed to be escaping her. The conversation was continuing between Mrs. Barton and Jonathan, who was carefully explaining about his father's death before the war and the plight of his mother and his sisters.

Grace's mind seemed to be locked in time. She was too stunned to move forward or backward. All along she had been certain that she could convince Jonathan to stay on at Riverwood; she hadn't been quite certain how she would do that, but believing that he loved her and knowing she loved him, she had expected their love to find a way.

As she walked beside Mrs. Barton on legs that felt as though they had turned to wood, she wondered if she had been mistaken all along about him. Maybe he didn't really love her after all; or if he did, maybe his feelings didn't go as deep as hers. If so, how could he just say good-bye to her here in Tuscaloosa and ride out of her life?

"Don't you think, Grace?"

Grace turned blank eyes to Jonathan, wondering what he had asked her. "Why don't we do some shopping and meet Mr. and Mrs. Barton in an hour for lunch at the tea room across the street?"

Grace followed his gaze across the street, and she heard herself agree. "Yes. Of course."

"Dear, I believe you stood out there in the sun too long. You look a little pale," Mrs. Barton said.

Grace felt Mrs. Barton's gloved hand upon hers, squeezing gently. She turned and looked into the kind woman's face and nodded. "Yes, I think so. We'll see you in an hour."

She had avoided looking at Jonathan for fear she would burst into tears. He had said good-bye to Mrs. Barton and placed his hand on her elbow to gently lead her into the coffee shop of the hotel.

She didn't say a word. She couldn't. It wasn't until they had taken a seat at a back table for privacy and Jonathan had ordered coffee that she felt the pressure of his hand on hers and forced herself to look at him.

His face was serious, and the blue eyes were bleak as he spoke. "I can see that you're upset. Is it because I have to leave?"

"Why?" The word sounded more like something she would have said as a child. Her voice was small and weak, and the word seemed lost in the abyss of her pain.

"Grace, you know I have to go back to Kentucky. I told you that from the very beginning, and I've done everything I can to help you." He hesitated.

The dining room was not crowded, and the waiter had quickly filled their coffee cups and was appearing at the table again.

Grace looked down at the white porcelain cup. The clear dark coffee sent a tiny breath of heat toward her. She needed the heat and the coffee to jolt her back to the person she had once been. All life seemed to have been drained from her there in the hot street with the awful announcement that Jonathan had made to Mrs. Barton.

She didn't respond until she had taken a sip of the coffee and felt the sting on her tongue. She didn't care that she had burned her tongue because she was too impatient to wait for it to cool down. Desperation pounded through her, and she knew she had to think clearly. With her strong will and sharp mind, she had found the best means of survival for her mother and herself. She had put to work the spirit her father had so often spoken about, and at times it had been the memory of her father's faith in that spirit, more than her own, that had kept her going.

Leaning back in the chair, she forced herself to look at Jonathan. She knew she had to be calm and not say anything she would regret. A deep, inner wisdom seemed to take over, refilling the void that had settled in her heart when she thought of Jonathan leaving. The panic that had overtaken her in the hot street had frightened her; she did not want to expose herself to that again, so she tried another approach.

"I understand your concern about your farm, Jonathan. And you know how appreciative my mother and I are to you for all that you've done. I guess I was just. . ." She dropped her gaze, watching her thumb nervously trace the rim of the cup handle. "Just surprised," she began again, "that since you were able to get a telegraph to your mother about being detained. . .well, I just thought you would get me safely back to Riverwood and say good-bye to Mother."

She paused, studying his face for the effect of her words. She had spoken the truth, but she knew as she did, she was also buying more time with him. She had to find a way to convince him to stay, and she felt sure that if he returned to Riverwood with her, he would not want to leave. And she hoped to talk her mother into helping her convince him to stay.

"But Grace, I don't see the necessity of my returning with you. I mean, since the Bartons are friends of your family, I feel confident that you will be safe with them. And they're going all the way back to Whites Creek. It seems like a perfectly sensible plan to me. Furthermore," he said, searching her eyes, "I think if you agree, your mother would understand. After all, she seemed very sympathetic to my situation."

Grace felt a slight twinge of temper but fought it down. "Just as I am sympathetic to your situation. But there's another reason." She paused, taking a sip of coffee, trying to think. She hated to stoop to using money as a means to an end, but she was still willing to share the money with him. After all, if he left with more money than planned, he might think the extra few days were worth his time.

"I don't feel right about only giving you two hundred dollars. You deserve more, and I can pay it. I intend to delay paying off my loan at Whites Creek until I get the farm in working order. Then Mr. Britton is more likely to advance money for next year if I need it, and I probably will. Jonathan, everything depends on getting a good cotton harvest. You've told me that. And I have no one to oversee any labor I hire. I don't have anyone to work the fields yet—"

"But Mr. Douglas and Reams will help you. And I'm certain Mr. Barton—"

She reached over and touched his arm. "If you will just help me hire some men and get them started, I won't ask you to stay any longer. And the money I would have used to pay the loan will go toward helping you meet your expenses when you return. Jonathan, for the sake of your family, you have to think of this more in a business manner."

He stared into her eyes, and as he did, something seemed to change in his face. He slipped his hand from hers and reached for his coffee cup, lifting it to take a sip. He watched her over the rim of the cup, and for a moment, Grace held her breath. She knew he was too smart to be fooled by feminine tricks, so she forced herself to think more about what she had just said to him, which did make sense. Why did he have to be so noble? If he needed money for his farm, and he obviously did, why wasn't he willing to take the money she had offered him?

"I didn't realize you were thinking of this in such a businesslike manner," he said.

Grace could hear a difference in his tone of voice, and she thought she knew what that meant. But she sensed that she had hit on the right approach, one that would work, although she wasn't sure she was going to like the ultimate result of her decision to turn this into a business deal.

"How else can I think of it?" she asked, looking him squarely in the eye. "And why are you willing to be so noble? You promised my mother and me that you would take me all the way to. . ." She looked around to make sure other customers could not hear their conversation. "All the way to our destination to accomplish our mission. I understood, and she did too, that you would get me safely back to Riverwood."

She glanced around and lowered her voice. "As for the Bartons, they are friends of ours." She looked back at Jonathan. "But they're even closer friends with the Brittons."

He leaned forward. "So are you saying that because of that friendship, you don't want them knowing your business?"

Grace nodded and made a point of glancing around the hotel coffee shop again. "Mr. Barton is much more shrewd than his wife. He's going to have a lot of questions about how I could obtain the horses and wagon and all the supplies we've bought."

"I can always say that I'm helping your family. For all they know, I could have advanced you money, could have brought money from your father. In a sense, that is exactly what has taken place."

As Grace listened, she studied his face and watched his eyes. Had he seen through her plan, or was he just testing her? Or was he merely pointing out a reasonable way to explain her money?

She nodded, studying her hands. "Yes, we could say that."

He waited for her to say more. When she did not, he touched her hand again. "The truth is, you feel that I am abandoning you, don't you, Grace?"

Her eyes shot back to him. "Yes, I do."

He sighed and shook his head wearily. "Grace, I wish there were an easy answer to this, but there isn't. I've been through four years of looking at the hard side of life, and I guess maybe I've become a bit cynical." He looked at her again. "I care for you. You know I do," he said softly. "But what chance do we have? Do you honestly think I can turn my back on my family and never go back?"

She shook her head quickly and found that she couldn't fight the tears in her eyes. "No, Jonathan, I would never want you to turn your back on your family, and of course, I want you to go back. I only wish I could go with you," she said, speaking the words before she even thought about them.

She was listening to her heart again, and this time her heart had spoken instead of her mind.

"You can," he said.

She blinked back the tears, touching her eyes with the corner of her lace handkerchief as he spoke the words. Then as the impact of what he had just said registered in her mind, she looked at him in surprise.

"You can go back with me," he repeated. "We haven't thought of that as a solution, but maybe it is."

She stared at him, her eyes still bleary from the tears.

"What do you mean?"

He shook his head and looked nervously around the room. "I'm not sure what I mean," he said.

As they sat in silence, trying to sort out their feelings, the thick drawl of southern voices flowed all around them, and for the first time, even Grace noticed the difference in the speech patterns. She had spent so much time listening to Jonathan the past week that to her the southern voices stood out.

Automatically, she glanced around her at the flow of people coming and going in the coffee shop. If they were sitting in a coffee shop in Louisville, the people would be listening to her voice and thinking she sounded different. And it would go further than that, she thought, as her eyes followed the figures of the various people, noticing how the contrast in their lives was paralleled in their clothing.

The better-dressed people she had seen were not Southerners but people like the couple they had met who had bought the plantation at Gordo. They were outsiders who had come in to buy up southern land. They were not *her* people. How could she, even for a minute, consider leaving Riverwood?

She would be a traitor to the South and to her own family to leave behind all that she was and who she was just to follow Jonathan back to Louisville.

"Jonathan, more people from. . .other areas. . .are coming to the South, whereas I don't believe you will find many of us in your area, buying land, or making friends with bankers and expanding their territory. Don't you see? It would be easier for you to stay here than for me to go there."

As she asked the question, she heard the conviction in her voice start to fade. Watching his face, she knew she had said the wrong thing, and she regretted it.

"Grace, I'm not staying here," he said. While he spoke in a quiet, even gentle tone of voice, Grace could not mistake the firmness in his voice. She knew he meant what he said.

"Then I guess we have nothing else to talk about."

What else could they say or do? They were both right. He couldn't live in Alabama; she couldn't live in Kentucky. Just as the war had dictated the course of events for their lives, the outcome of that conflict was changing the course of her life in ways she had not even begun to comprehend.

She started to get up from the chair, and Jonathan stood as well. She knew he was watching her closely, and she avoided his eyes for a moment as she waged a battle with her conscience. She sighed. She had lost the battle to hang onto him, if only for another week or two. She had almost resigned herself to the fact that she would become an old maid and grow old and die at Riverwood alone. She had been living in a dream world to think that would change.

"Grace, I don't want to hurt you," Jonathan said, as he came around the table to stand beside her. "That's the last thing in the world I want to do."

She nodded as she looked up into his eyes. "I know, and I believe you," she said, relieved not to be trying to be so businesslike or playing any silly games with him.

"It's time to go meet the Bartons. What do you want to tell them?"

She took a deep breath. Again, she reached deep in her soul for the strength that always seemed to reside there when she really needed it. She prayed she could be strong now, for saying good-bye to Jonathan Parker would be the most difficult thing she had ever done.

"I'll go with them," she said, as she began to walk toward the door. "And you're free to go on to Kentucky."

eleven

Grace and Jonathan soon reached the yellow frame house with gingerbread trim. It was a cozy two-story home, and the first floor had been converted to a tea room to support the small family who now resided on the upper floor.

The front parlors held four, linen-covered tables surrounded by cushioned, straight-backed chairs in each room, accommodating a total of thirty-two guests. A love seat and coffee table provided a space for two people, but a couple with a little girl had nestled into the love seat and ordered sandwiches and tea.

All the tables were taken, but Grace quickly spotted Mrs. Barton waving from a table where she and her husband were seated with two extra chairs reserved for Grace and Jonathan.

They walked over to the table, and Mr. Barton stood up to greet them. Mrs. Barton was smiling in her reassuring way that always put Grace at ease.

Mr. Barton was a small man with a sturdy build and a friendly round face and dark hair. His dark eyes were fixed on Jonathan with a look of interest as he extended his hand. After the introductions were made and Grace and Jonathan had taken their seats, Mr. Barton opened the conversation.

"My wife has been telling me how kind you've been to Grace and Elizabeth," he said. "And Fred. . ." He faltered on the word and looked down for a moment. "Fred was one of the finest men in the county," he continued, looking at Grace. "His family meant the world to him. He and I were together right here in Tuscaloosa when we read the list of casualties at the town hall and saw Freddy's name."

He shook his head and looked at his wife, as though needing her strength. She smiled sadly at him and reached out to pat his hand. "Mildred and I lost two babies and were grateful for our two daughters later in life. I couldn't begin to imagine the tragedy Fred felt that day when he saw his only son had lost his life."

Grace looked at Jonathan and saw that he appeared to be mesmerized by Mr. Barton and the sad story he was relating.

Mr. Barton looked at his wife and said nothing for a moment.

Mrs. Barton turned to Grace. "Dear, I can only say that as horrible as it has been for your parents to lose Freddy, it must be almost unbearable for Elizabeth to know that Fred isn't coming back to her."

She turned and looked at Jonathan. "How good of you to be so loyal to Fred and now to his family. You must be a very special man," she said, giving him the full radiance of her smile.

Jonathan seemed to have lost his voice for a moment. He merely gave her a sad smile in return, then looked across at Grace.

"It has been my honor and privilege to know Mr. Cunningham then his wife. And Grace. I only wish I could do more for them."

As she and Jonathan looked at one another, Mr. Barton resumed the conversation. "And now Mildred tells me you are going on to Kentucky."

Jonathan slowly turned his attention to the Bartons. "I will be going back to Kentucky soon," he said. "But after talking with Grace, I have decided to see her safely back to Riverwood and say good-bye to her mother."

Grace gasped so loudly that she was certain the Bartons had heard. For a moment, no one said anything, but Mrs. Barton tactfully responded. "Well, I'm relieved to hear you say that. I must confess, I was worried that Grace would tire of our visiting relatives, but we had already promised."

"I took the liberty of checking on the condition of the river myself," Mr. Barton said. "I spoke with some people who had just come into town last night, and they confirmed what Mr. Sawyers told you. I think he is correct in the route he suggested. Furthermore, I don't believe you'll have a long wait, or rather I hope you won't. Since this is a Tuesday, it's not likely to be as crowded on the ferry as it would be if it were the weekend."

Jonathan nodded in agreement, and Grace sneaked another glance in his direction.

"That's good to hear, Sir. We're purchasing some groceries, then we should get on our way. Do you mind if we don't stay for lunch?" Jonathan asked, directing the question more to Mrs. Barton.

"Of course not. In fact, I think you're wise to be on your way."

Mr. Barton stood again as Jonathan came around to assist Grace from her chair.

"Let me again express my appreciation to you, young man. And when I get back next week, if you're still in our parts, we insist on you two coming for dinner." He looked at Grace. "If Elizabeth is up to a visit, we would love to see her as well."

"Thank you, Mr. Barton."

She leaned over to hug him, then she bent down to hug Mrs. Barton. She didn't know how to thank them for being so kind and gracious to her and of course to Jonathan. They had innocently worked the miracle that she had been unable to attain. Jonathan would stay awhile longer.

As they said good-bye again and walked out of the tea room, Grace looked up at Jonathan. "You don't have to take me back. I don't want anyone to make you feel that you do. And I won't do that to you again," she said, her voice trembling.

She still felt bad about trying to talk him into staying by using money as an argument, and yet she meant to give him the money she had originally promised. She fully intended to carry out her plan of delaying her payment to Mr. Britton at the bank in the interest of getting the farm up and going again.

"Oh, Grace, I can't just leave you like this," he said, sighing. "You were right. Another week isn't going to make that much difference, after all. And I realize now that I would always feel that I hadn't finished what I had promised your father I would do if I didn't see for myself that you and your mother were going to be okay when I leave."

When I leave. The words drummed in her mind on the way back to the store to get more food. Still, she had decided to be more reasonable about everything. At least she would have Jonathan with her for another week, and he was right. They were still in desperate need of his help. For the moment, she was afraid to trust anyone but Jonathan.

She slipped her hand in his. "Thank you, Jonathan."

After buying more supplies, they climbed up on the wagon and headed west. True to Mr. Sawyer's prediction, the road was well traveled, although not overly crowded with people. At least there had been enough traffic to keep the road maintained, and occasionally people waved to them or even offered water when they stopped to rest.

It was almost dark when at last Jonathan and Grace reached the tent settlement that had sprung up around the ferry. Their hopes for a short wait before crossing on the ferry were quickly dashed. Wagons were lined up, backed up, and spread around a grove of oaks where people had set up rough campsites while they waited.

"Oh no," Jonathan moaned as he pushed back his hat and looked around the group.

Grace felt a knot of apprehension upon seeing the crowd,

and she wondered if they had made a mistake.

They pulled the wagon into the grove of oaks and got out to see to the horses tied on to the rear of the wagon. Jonathan hesitated, and when Grace glanced from his face to the crowd, she saw the reason.

Unlike the agreeable Bartons, who had given them such optimism, the people who waited to catch the ferry were a different breed. They had worn-out faces, wore old work clothes, looked tired, and spoke in coarse voices using rough language. Two men were on the brink of a fight not far from the wagon, and Grace quickly walked away upon hearing the names and insults flying back and forth.

The entire scene brought to mind their encounter with Sonny, and a chill ran over her even though the heat was miserable, and her perspiration-soaked clothes were sticking to her in places.

She turned to Jonathan. "Let's go."

He scanned the crowd, saying nothing, his hands in his pockets. Even though he was dressed in riding clothes, he stood out in the crowd as a gentleman, and Grace was terrified of what might happen if someone drew them into conversation. Some of these characters would welcome a chance to vent their frustration on a Yankee, and she and Jonathan were practically defenseless against such a crowd.

Jonathan looked down at her and shook his head. "We'll stay," he said in a low voice. He took her arm, and they walked quietly away from the disgruntled people to a secluded stretch of meadow.

"I counted the people waiting, and it looks like we could board the ferry by noon tomorrow, once we get in line. I think our best bet is to stay to ourselves, bed down early, then hope the line moves fast in the morning."

Grace frowned, glancing back at the array of slab-ribbed mules, wagons with tattered canvas, and a few tired-looking horses. "Jonathan, I don't feel good about this. I think we should leave."

"Grace, look at the sky. It'll be dark before we travel two miles. And I'd rather take our chances camped here with people than on our own back there on the road. At least we can see who's around us here, and who knows? Maybe you can make friends with some of the women."

Grace thought about his words and studied the crowd once more, wondering who would want to be friends with her. "Jonathan, I'm not too tired to ride back to Tuscaloosa if you're willing."

He sighed. "That isn't safe or sensible. I think the smartest thing to do is stay put and keep to ourselves."

"Then promise me something," she said, placing her hands on his chest and looking up into his eyes.

"What's that?" The look of worry slipped away from his face as he gathered her hands in his and searched her face.

"Promise me that we *will* stay to ourselves. I don't want another fight like the one with Sonny."

He chuckled, glancing back at the group. "Neither do I. There isn't a sheriff here to come to our rescue. Somehow I don't think I'd win this fight."

Grace nodded. "I'm going to say that you're sick. That way you can stay apart from the group."

"If they think I'm sick, I imagine they'll want to stay away from me. But don't put yourself in a position that requires me to come to your defense."

"I won't. I promise."

Grace was so relieved that she smiled. And when she remembered what he had said about coming to her defense, she knew he meant it.

She tiptoed up to plant a kiss on his cheek. "I love you, Jonathan Parker," she said, then hurried off before he could respond.

It was the first time she had told him how she felt, but she no longer wished to keep her feelings to herself. She wanted him to know the truth.

As she sauntered back to the group, Grace began to look them over carefully. To her relief, the two rude men had been separated, and one was riding off on his horse.

"And don't come back," another man yelled after him.

She frowned, watching the man disappear in a cloud of dust over the road they had just traveled. Soon the men had dispersed in different directions. Two walked back to the wagons parked nearest to her own.

She stopped at her wagon and sorted through her purchases. She found the peppermint sticks she had purchased to take home and decided it was time to do some trading: candy for friendship. Pushing a smile onto her weary face, she set out for the nearest wagon.

An older woman knelt beside the ashes of a campfire. She was peeling potatoes into a big pot. Grace walked up and introduced herself with the intent of learning something about her neighbors. She soon discovered that the Adam Smith family was from Perry County. They were on their way to buy land near Tupelo, Mississippi.

"Our place was worn out before the war," Mrs. Smith told Grace. "I got an older brother settled in Tupelo. He sent word there was land near him."

Grace smiled. "I've heard Tupelo is nice."

As they continued their conversation, Grace realized this family had been on the road for days, and the rumpled clothing and tired faces were more a result of their long trip than any other reason. She learned that two of the wagons belonged to the Smiths, along with several horses, a milk cow, and two yearling calves.

In a field away from the wagons, Grace could see children playing. Mrs. Smith pointed out their two sons and a daughter who were with the group in the field. Their seventeen-year-old son, Tom, was just leaving with his father to gather firewood. A little boy was asleep in the wagon. Grace left the candy and proceeded to the next wagon.

Mrs. Smith had told her the Joe Wheeler family was traveling with them as far as Memphis. When Grace stopped to chat with Jane Wheeler, she could see the Wheelers were quite poor, but the woman was gracious to her, and Grace regretted judging them so quickly.

"Everyone seems nice," Grace remarked, handing the Wheeler's young son, Roby, a peppermint.

"Just watch out for those folk." Jane pointed toward a wagon parked by itself on the edge of the pasture. "That man's brother was the one that just got run off for trying to steal something outa the first wagon down there."

"Thank you for telling me," Grace said.

As she studied the isolated wagon, she could make out a heavyset woman with red hair tied up in braids on top of her head. The woman was stomping around the back of the wagon, dragging cooking pots out of a trunk while yelling at a small redheaded girl playing in the dirt.

"They got three more girls, all look just like their mother. And the husband—don't know where he is now—he's a drinker. Joe says he reckon he has to stay drunk to put up with the wife and girls. They only got one voice, and it's loud, from daylight to dark."

Grace laughed at the colorful description, but she didn't forget the warning to stay away from the man. She wanted to be certain Jonathan was warned.

"Well, I'll be getting back to my wagon. Jonathan is sick, and I've told him he shouldn't be around other people while he's not well."

"No, we don't want our kids getting sick."

"I know, but it was nice meeting you," Grace said with

a smile, then hurried back to her wagon. She felt a lot better about the people who were camping around them. Now all they had to do was stay to themselves, as Jonathan had suggested.

Staying to themselves was easy enough for the first part of the night. But when the lanterns were being extinguished and people were settling down to sleep, the first threat of trouble appeared.

After dark, Grace had made her bed inside the wagon, and Jonathan had pitched his bedroll outside. They had been talking in low voices to each other for about a half hour when they heard a child scream.

Grace crawled to the back of the wagon and looked out. Jonathan was already on his feet, staring toward the wagon on the edge of the pasture.

Grace followed his gaze and saw a lantern swinging precariously from its perch as a man backed against the canvas, his fists doubled. He stared down at the woman on the ground.

He was muttering something they couldn't hear as the woman kicked at him, and he kicked back.

Grace gasped, appalled by what was taking place. She had never seen a man and woman fight, but it was obvious the man was being a bully.

"Why isn't someone going over to stop him?" Jonathan asked, taking a few steps forward.

Grace's arm shot out, grabbing his sleeve. "Jonathan, we aren't going to get into this," she said, yanking even harder when it appeared he was about to take another step. She could see his tall profile silhouetted in the moonlight, and as she kept her grip on his arm and climbed out of the wagon, his face became more distinct. The muscle in his jaw started to clench.

He yanked his arm loose. "I'm not going to cower over

here while a man beats a woman."

Just then a child cried out, and Grace and Jonathan watched in horror as one of the girls came out of the wagon, screaming and yelling at her father. She pulled at his sleeve as the woman crawled around in the dirt, then the man swung around and backhanded the girl, sending her flying into the grass.

Grace wrapped her arms around Jonathan, pleading with him as he started to move beneath her weight. "No, please, Jonathan. I'm begging you. Don't go over there," she sobbed, desperate to make him listen.

"Grace, what kind of person do you think I am? I'm not going to stand here and watch that bully beat a woman and child and do nothing about it."

"But you'll end up—"

"In a fight? I don't care."

He charged across the meadow. Grace stood rooted to the spot, watching in horror. Then she started running to catch up with him, hoping she could somehow intervene. But she wasn't fast enough, for Jonathan reached the man just as his fist swung out again. He hadn't seen Jonathan's approach, so Jonathan was able to grab the man's fist and haul him backward. Without saying a word, Jonathan flattened the man with two blows, while the girls screamed behind them and the lantern went flying from the wagon across the grass.

By the time Grace got to them, Adam Smith and his oldest son were running across the meadow, yelling something to Jonathan.

Just then the redheaded woman came up behind Jonathan, her arm swinging.

In the eerie light of the lantern, Grace saw a silver flash as the woman struck Jonathan's arm. His elbow swung back, knocking her away, before he even knew who was fighting him.

"Hold it," Adam warned, pointing a rifle at the man on the

ground. "Tom, grab the woman," he ordered his son, who towered above all the other men.

Tom stepped forward and grasped the woman by her arms. She screamed at Jonathan while the man on the ground cursed and threatened to kill him. The girls jumped up and down, screaming at the top of their lungs.

It was the worst scene Grace had ever witnessed, but as the other men in the camp took over, Jane Wheeler extended a piece of cloth to Jonathan. "Here, put this on your arm."

Jonathan pressed the cloth against his arm and turned and walked back toward their wagon.

Grace stared after him, still sobbing and trembling. Two of the other women reached out to comfort her.

"Go on back with him," Jane said, standing beside Grace. "We'll manage here. It's not a deep cut," she added, patting Grace's shoulder. "I could see that when I handed him the cloth.

Grace nodded and plodded back toward the wagon. She felt sick after what she had just witnessed. The ugly scene and the terror that had seized her when she saw the cut on Jonathan's arm had left her weak. By the time she reached the wagon, waves of nausea rolled over her.

As she bent over double and began to retch, she felt an arm around her waist. Then Jonathan handed her a cup of cold water.

Drinking the water slowly, Grace felt her stomach settle. Jonathan led her back to the wagon, where he had lit the lantern. As she crawled up to the wagon bed, she realized he had released her and was stepping back. She looked over her shoulder, seeing in the glow of the lantern the dark look in his eyes.

"Get some sleep," he said and turned away.

"Jonathan, your arm—"

"I'm okay."

Her fear drifted away, and suddenly her numb temper came to life. He still stood in the shadows, pressing the cloth to his arm.

"Why did you have to go over there? The other men were on their way. They didn't need you."

He stepped out of the shadows and stood with his face only inches from hers. His eyes filled with anger, and his voice was tightly controlled. "I have never tucked my tail and run, and I'm not going to now. If you think that I'm going to cower down because I'm a Yank and everybody hates me, then you don't know me at all. I'll get you home, then I'm leaving this country. You see—this is the way it would be if I had allowed you to talk me into staying on. I'd rather have died in the war than be only half a man, and that's what you seem to expect of me. Well, I'm not going to do that, Grace."

He turned and stomped off around the side of the wagon, and Grace sat back on her heel, reeling with shock. She had never seen him so angry; the only time he had lost his temper was the day Sonny had challenged him. But now he was acting like a hotheaded soldier who couldn't stop fighting a war or a southerner.

"Jonathan Parker," she yelled through the canvas. "Get on your horse and go to Kentucky. I can get home by myself."

Her cry of rage seemed to resonate into the distant shadows, but there was no response. She flung herself down on the quilts and began to sob. A sick feeling began to gather in the pit of her stomach, but she knew she would rather choke before going outside to throw up again. She buried her face into the feather pillow and sobbed harder. Once she had muffled her own cries, she could hear low voices in the night, and she put her hand over her mouth and strained to hear.

Two men were talking as they approached the wagon. She sat up, terror rolling over her again.

"They're pulling out now," Adam Smith was saying. "We told them if they didn't leave now, we were sending Jeb for the sheriff in Tuscaloosa. Reckon they must have something to hide, 'cause they got real quiet then. They're breaking camp. The woman thinks you're hurt worse than you are, and we didn't tell 'em different. So you just lie low till they're gone."

Grace scrambled toward the back of the wagon. "Thank you," she called out. "We appreciate it."

The Smith boy held a lantern, and she could see more men in the background.

"Thank you, Sir," Jonathan said in a loud, clear voice. "I never could tolerate a man mistreating a woman."

She held her breath. She suspected that he had deliberately spoken up to let them know he was a Yankee. Now what would happen?

"Nope, I never could tolerate that either," Mr. Smith replied. "Come on, men. Let's get back to the wagon."

Grace watched Jonathan turn and stride toward her. He looked angrier than before. "I'm glad not everyone is as worried about my voice as you are. I heard you tell me to leave, but I'll see you safely home. Then I'll be glad to go."

He disappeared around the side of the wagon, and she fell back on the quilt, exhausted. She was beyond tears, beyond anger. She lay in the darkness, listening to the low voices melt away in the distance. She closed her eyes, but she knew she wouldn't sleep.

Much later, she heard the creak of a wagon and the plod of horses, and she sat up and peered through the back of the wagon. Two men stood by the road with lanterns. One had a rifle pointed at the wagon as it rocked off down the road. For the first time, the entire family was silent, and Grace wondered if their silence was even more threatening than their menacing shouts.

twelve

Neither Jonathan nor Grace spoke the next morning as Jonathan tied the horses onto the back of the wagon, and Grace folded her quilts and tidied up. She hadn't slept more than two hours, and even then, her sleep had been riddled with nightmares of the redheaded woman bearing down on her with a knife, then the redheaded girls chasing her across the meadow, all screaming and lunging at her as they caught up.

Grace knew she had made too much fuss about their wild neighbors. Still, as they lined up with the others to get on the ferry, it was obvious that Jonathan had chosen to ignore her. He was still angry at her, but she didn't care. She was just as angry at him.

They boarded the ferry with the other families, and Grace was immensely relieved to be able to talk with the other women. It gave her an excuse to avoid Jonathan until they reached the other side of the river.

Once they did, she climbed up on the wagon and turned her head away from Jonathan. She was almost as angry at herself as she was with him. What had happened to her spirit? In the past, she would have called his bluff first thing in the morning. She would have told him again that she could manage on her own. Yet here she was saying nothing, and that gave the impression she was pouting, which was not her style. But she couldn't prod her temper enough to fuss with him, nor evoke her independent spirit to the point of dismissing him, so she sulked most of the day, and he pretended that he was alone.

Finally, after hours on the trail, Jonathan pulled the wagon into a shady grove and drew back on the horses. Pulling on the brake, he tied the reins and hopped down.

Grace sneaked a glance toward him and saw he had the water bucket and was headed toward a line of trees that probably lined a stream. Slowly, she climbed down from the wagon. Dragging herself to the rear she petted the horses and untied Lucky. She walked the mare over to some thick grass and tethered her to a hickory sapling. Then she went back for Banjo.

"I'm glad you two get along so well," she murmured to the horse. It amazed her that she and Jonathan had so completely ruined the good relationship that once existed. Sinking down into a cool, shady area under the trees, she drew her knees up to her chin and put her head down. She had no idea how to remedy the situation, and she reminded herself it was probably useless to try. He was determined to see her safely home, then leave. She should be glad; it would be easier for everyone when he was gone.

The smell of smoke caused her to jump to her feet, wincing at her sore muscles. She ran back out into the clearing so she could check the wagon. Jonathan had built a low fire and was cooking something. Fine, let him eat; she wasn't hungry. She strolled back over to see about the horses, and as she did, her gaze met Jonathan's, and he called out to her.

"I'm warming some food."

"I'm not hungry."

He stood up and began to walk in her direction. She turned back to the horses, thinking he was probably coming over in the interest of the horses, rather than her.

"Look, Grace," he said as he stopped walking and stood regarding her from a dozen yards away. "We'll be back at your place by dark. I think we'd better settle this and not upset your mother."

She looked at him, wondering what there was to settle.

"Well, you will have kept your word when we get there, so feel free to leave whenever you want."

He turned and looked to the west, in the direction they would be traveling. "All right, I'll do that."

With narrowed eyes, Grace watched him stalk back to the fire. What had she expected? Deep in her heart, she thought if she remained cool and aloof, he would give in and say something. But she had underestimated his degree of stubbornness. He was his own man, one not easily maneuvered, or maybe one who would not be maneuvered at all.

She went back to stroke Lucky's forehead. "I guess I wanted a man who could stand on his own feet," she whispered. "But maybe I didn't know that. Now it's too late." And she pressed her face against Lucky's forehead.

Jonathan had been right in his estimation of when they'd arrive at Riverwood. It had been a sunny day, but soon twilight would filter over the land. When Grace saw familiar landmarks, she felt a surge of joy. Suddenly she wanted to make peace with Jonathan.

"Thank you for getting me there and back. And for everything else," she said, turning her head slightly so that she barely looked at him.

"You're welcome."

She swallowed. He wasn't going to say anything more. "How does your arm feel? The cut, I mean."

"It's okay. I got into our medicine kit and bandaged it up before I went to bed."

Guilt tore at her conscience, and her reserve crumpled. "Jonathan, I'm so sorry. I've acted like a spoiled child. I should have bandaged your arm, cooked for you, or just. . . behaved differently. I'm so sorry," she said, and for a moment, she feared she would burst into tears.

He looked at her and smiled. "I forgive you, Grace. And I'm sorry too."

They had made their peace just in time, for Jonathan was turning the wagon up the drive to home. Grace couldn't wait to see her mother and tell her all that had happened. As soon as they rounded the curve, she saw her mother sitting on the porch, waiting as she always did. Upon seeing them, Elizabeth stood up and walked to the edge of the porch, gripping the post with one hand.

"Hi, Mother," Grace called. "How do you like the new wagon?"

Grace watched as her mother put a hand to her mouth and began to giggle like a young girl. Suddenly, Grace was laughing too, and so was Jonathan.

Grace jumped down from the wagon almost before Jonathan had pulled the horses to a halt, then she ran up the steps to hug her mother.

"Come into the kitchen. I have a meal waiting for you," Elizabeth said after the three had exchanged greetings.

Grace watched her curiously. From the way her mother looked, Grace thought she somehow understood everything that had taken place.

"I'll take care of the horses and put the wagon away," Jonathan said, smiling as Grace and her mother walked arm in arm back inside the house.

Once they were in the kitchen, Grace sat down with her mother at the table and told her the full story. Elizabeth did not seem as surprised as Grace expected, although she smiled and hugged Grace from time to time. When Grace finished the long story, carefully omitting her fight with Jonathan and the reason for it, she studied her mother curiously.

"Mother, you don't seem astounded by all this. To me, this is like the most wonderful dream I could ever imagine, but it's really happened. Can you believe it?"

Her mother smiled, and tears began to form in her hazel eyes. "Of course I am surprised and overjoyed. But I always knew God would work things out. I just didn't know how He would do it."

Grace stared at her, saying nothing for a moment. Then she too felt the rush of tears, and she let them flow freely down her cheeks. "Mother, I love you," she said. "You have been so strong in your faith. I'll never forget the lesson you have taught me."

They sat in the kitchen, hugging one another and crying, marveling at all the blessings that had come to them. Then Jonathan's steps sounded in the hall, and Grace got up to help her mother take the meal to the dining-room table.

They talked as they ate, and once or twice Grace smiled warmly at Jonathan. She had forgotten her anger and the words that had been spoken in haste, and she only hoped that Jonathan had as well.

It had been a long day, and by the time they finished their meal, darkness had settled over the house. Grace was so tired she almost hadn't noticed that her mother went about lighting the candles.

"You look absolutely exhausted," Jonathan said, his elbow on the table.

She smiled at him. Dark circles lined his eyes, and the shadow of a beard covered his jaw. "So do you. I think we've earned a good night's sleep."

He nodded and got up slowly. "I didn't realize until now that I'm practically asleep on my feet." He stretched his arms over his head, then winced.

"Jonathan, your shoulder," Grace said, worried again.

"It's healing fine. I washed off down at the watering trough when I was seeing to the horses. I checked the cut place then, and I'm strong as ever." He winked at her. "Get a good night's rest. First thing in the morning, I want to ride over and see Mr. Douglas and ask about getting you some fieldhands."

She nodded. "Thank you, Jonathan." As she looked across at him, she wanted to say more, so much more, but she knew she was far too tired to make sense. "I'll see you in the morning. Rest well."

He had started to walk around the table to her side when her mother entered the dining room again. Grace suspected that Jonathan wanted to kiss her, but he was still mindful of his promise to her mother.

Elizabeth looked at Jonathan. "I've prepared the guest room for you. I pray you sleep well."

"I will," he said and patted her arm. "Good night."

Soon after Jonathan had gone upstairs, Grace left her mother in the parlor and trudged up to her own room. When she settled into her soft bed, she moaned with relief. She was glad to be home; she hoped she never had to leave again.

❧

Grace was seated on the front porch, enjoying her second cup of coffee, when Jonathan rode back up the drive, returning from a visit to the Douglas place. Her mother had just come to the door to say she had most of the supplies put away.

Grace only half heard what her mother said as she watched Jonathan walk up to the front porch. She thought about what a handsome man he was, but she knew so many more important things about him now, his kindness, his loyalty, and his honesty. He was every bit as bound to duty and honor as her father had been.

"Mr. Douglas told me to go down to the dock at Jina and ask for a man named Isaac Banks. He's working at the docks, but he wants to get back to farming," Jonathan said as he settled lazily into a chair beside her.

Watching him, Grace noticed how at ease he seemed to be. Hope sprang in her heart. Maybe now that they were back at Riverwood, he would change his mind. She wasn't going to try to persuade him not to go to Kentucky; she had learned her lesson about that. But she dared hope that somehow they could work out a plan.

"Someone told Mr. Douglas that Isaac didn't like having to live on the docks, that he wants to move back to the country. He is said to be the best worker in the county."

Grace tried to follow the conversation, reminding herself that she should be paying closer attention. "Jina is only an hour's ride," she answered. "Would you want to go and talk with this man?" she asked, feeling a bit shy about requesting anything more of him.

Jonathan nodded. "I can, but since you're the one who's hiring him, I think you should go along so he understands who the boss is."

Grace averted her eyes. She had promised herself that she was not going to argue with Jonathan. She was so happy over all their blessings that she couldn't stir up any independent feelings.

"Yes, Grace, why don't you go with him?" her mother suggested.

Glancing over her shoulder, Grace realized that her mother had again assumed the responsibility of meals, freeing Grace to think of business. "Okay, I'll be ready in a minute."

She hurried upstairs to change clothes, and when she returned, Jonathan had saddled Banjo and Lucky. She stood for a moment, stroking first one horse, then the other. "Jonathan, I'm so grateful to have a good horse."

"I know. I thought I'd try Banjo and give General a rest."

As they rode down the drive, Grace continued stroking Lucky and looked over at Banjo. "They make a great pair, don't they?"

At his hesitation, Grace looked across and saw that Jonathan was watching her differently. The twinkle had returned to his eyes, and he was smiling at her. "Yep, a good pair."

She returned his smile, and as they rode on, Grace thought

she had never in her life felt such happiness.

They reached Jina in less than an hour. The little settlement was nestled on a high bank overlooking the Tombigbee River. It bustled with activity as workers loaded freight from the dock to be shipped downriver to Mobile.

Securing their horses at the hitching post, they headed toward the small huts where the workers lived. Mr. Douglas had said Isaac lived in the first cabin on the right. As they approached the cabin, a deep bass voice belted out one of Grace's favorite songs: *"Weep no more, my lady. . .oh, weep no more, I pray. . ."*

The door of the cabin opened, and a huge black man stepped out. He was dressed in work clothes, a brown felt hat riding low on his broad forehead.

"Hello," Jonathan called to him. "We're looking for Isaac Banks."

"Afternoon. I'm Isaac." He removed his hat, revealing thick gray hair. In a mere half dozen steps, he caught up with them and stood towering over the couple. Grace thought he was the biggest man she had ever seen. She judged him to be at least six feet, five inches, all muscles and brawn, weighing at least 250 pounds. He had large, blunt features and a grim expression in his dark eyes.

Grace felt Jonathan's eyes on her, and she cleared her throat. "I'm Grace Cunningham. I understand you're looking for work."

"Yes'm."

"Mr. Paul Douglas sent me to see if you'd be willing to come to work for us at Riverwood," she continued.

He began to twist the worn brim of his felt hat in his large hands as he looked from Grace to Jonathan, then back again. "Are you goin' to try and grow cotton again?" he asked. "I ain't never gonna pick cotton again."

Grace heard the bitterness in his voice, and she remembered

Mr. Douglas had said that this man had spent his life working cotton. He was a fierce man, she could see that, and she wanted to be sure she made her plan clear to him.

"I'm not asking you to pick cotton," she replied gently. "If we grow cotton, I would put you in charge of the other men as my overseer."

"She's interested in clearing off the fields first," Jonathan explained. "The fields haven't been farmed in a few years, so they'll need to be cleaned up and burned over."

"I don't mind doing that," Isaac answered, "but I won't pick cotton."

"Fair enough," Grace agreed.

"I make a dollar a day working at the docks," he said, still looking doubtful.

"I'll pay you that," Grace offered firmly.

"But I'd need to stay at the docks a few more days," he said. "I can't just up and quit and leave them shorthanded."

"I understand. Do you think you could come in about a week?"

"Yes'm." He clamped his hat on his head. "I reckon I can do that. You're the farm next the Mr. Douglas's place?"

"That's right. My father was Fred Cunningham."

He nodded. "He was a good fair man."

"Thank you, Isaac. If you want advance pay—"

"I don't take nothing till I've earned it."

"All right. Then I'll see you in a few days."

"Yes'm." He clapped his felt hat low on his forehead and struck a path toward the docks.

Grace looked at Jonathan. "I think he's exactly the kind of man I need to oversee the cotton."

Jonathan nodded. "I agree. Well, this was easy enough. Shall we go back now?"

They talked and laughed all the way back to Riverwood, and Grace was in high spirits as they rode back up the drive.

Then, she saw the fancy carriage parked in the driveway with its familiar family crest on the side of the carriage door. The driver sat under an oak tree, staring out at the pasture.

"That's the Britton carriage," Grace said, looking at Jonathan. She wondered what its presence could mean. If Mr. Britton had come calling, concerned about the money she owed, then she had some wonderful news for him.

She smiled to herself and looked over at Jonathan. "Come on inside. I want you to meet Mr. Britton. He's a very nice man."

As soon as they stepped into the hall, Grace realized it was not Mr. Britton who had come to call, but rather his wife, who was considered the town snob.

"I must say, Elizabeth, I'm shocked that you would allow such a thing." Her high-pitched voice reached Grace, and she felt as though she had just drawn her fingernails over rusty iron.

Grace turned to Jonathan. "Maybe you'd better excuse us. If you want to go on to the barn with the horses, I'll be down in a minute," she whispered, leaving Jonathan in the hall.

As Grace hurried into the parlor, Mrs. Britton whirled from the love seat, fluttering the feather in her hat. The little hat slid lower on the woman's broad, silver head, and she turned to Grace with a sharp look that sliced her up and down.

"Grace, Eva Nell Douglas told me you left your mother all alone and went off with. . .that man."

"No, it wasn't like that," Elizabeth said.

"Mr. Britton and I have been hearing all sorts of things," the woman continued, gathering momentum with each word. "I understand your *houseguest* brawled in the streets with some character, and it took Sheriff Whitworth to break it up. Mrs. Primrose says you are quite friendly with this. . .this *Yankee*. Really, Grace, what are you thinking of after your father and your brother—"

Elizabeth rose to her feet, looking with contempt at Mrs. Britton. "Samantha, you have completely misconstrued the facts. Jonathan Parker is here at my invitation because he saved Fred's life—"

"Don't be gullible, Elizabeth. Naturally, he would say that. How else would he weasel his way into Riverwood? They're after southern land, you know, all of them."

Grace was so angry she forced herself to mentally count to ten before she opened her mouth. But she saw that Mrs. Britton was reaching for her purse, ready to run after her insulting little speech.

"Mrs. Britton, Jonathan Parker has a farm of his own and has no need of ours. He—"

"You can comfort yourself with that idea, Grace, but no one believes it. Furthermore, you may not have a farm much longer if you don't repay your debt to the bank. My husband has been concerned about this all along; but in view of your behavior of late, it now appears that you could get swindled out of what Fred worked so hard to give you. We intend to see that such an event doesn't happen," she said, pausing at the door to sneer at Grace again.

Her mother stood beside Grace, her hand on her arm. She could feel her mother's message: Don't say anything more.

So Grace kept her silence. She swallowed back her fury and waited until she heard the sound of the driver calling to the horses and the wheels of the carriage rolling down the driveway.

"Mother, forget what she said," Grace cried. "I'll see Mr. Britton first thing in the morning and straighten this out."

She turned and headed toward the stairs, venting her anger with quick steps up the stairway. She would rush down to the barn and join Jonathan with the horses. She would forget. . .

At the top of the stairs, her eyes widened as she saw Jonathan close the door to the guest room and walk down the hall, his small traveling satchel in his hand.

She stared at him. "What are you doing?"

"I'm leaving, Grace."

He hurried past her and down the stairs before she could summon a response. She turned and looked after him as he strode down the hall toward the back door.

She flew down the stairs after him, her mind working. He obviously had not gone to the barn; instead, he had lingered in the hall out of concern, and he had heard every ugly word Mrs. Britton had spoken.

Well, she would explain. She would persuade him to stay overnight and talk things out.

He was already out the door, his long legs moving swiftly toward the pasture where General grazed.

"Jonathan, wait." She ran after him, catching up at the end of the yard. "Everyone knows Mrs. Britton is an ugly gossip who treats everyone unfairly. You can't let her words—"

"Some of the things she said made sense, Grace, even though you may not want to admit it. Those people have no way of knowing who I am or what my motives are. They only have my word—"

"Which is more than enough. Why, when Mr. Barton gets back—"

"At this moment, the bank owns Riverwood," Jonathan continued sternly. "You can't afford to ruffle Britton's feathers, Grace. Once you've paid him back, you can say what you want to his wife. Which brings up another point. I am still determined not to take any more of your money. You can't afford not to pay back that loan now, Grace. You have to."

Grace stood speechless, knowing deep in her heart that he was right. If she gave him as much money as she had offered, she would have to wait until the cotton harvest to repay the loan. Assuming there was a cotton harvest.

She swallowed, reaching out to restrain him as he turned to

go. She knew she was losing him; it would take more than money or desperate pleas to stop him now. All she had left was the bare truth, and as he turned briefly to face her, she knew she had to give him that.

"I won't beg you to stay, but you must know this. I love you, Jonathan. Nothing can change that; nothing ever will." She looked him straight in the eye and saw his eyes brighten. She even thought he was beginning to smile.

But the smile faded as he reached for her, pulling her close to his chest. "And I love you, Grace. God only knows how hard I've tried to talk myself out of it, but it's no use. You've been honest with me when I know it must have been difficult. What's even more difficult is that I can't stay here, Grace. I have to return to Kentucky."

He hesitated, glancing over her shoulder as though considering something. Then he pulled her closer to him, hugging her against his chest as though he never wanted to let her go. "Come with me. Please. We can be happy together, I know we can. We both love horses, and we can make our dreams come true in Kentucky. Come with me, and we'll build a new life together in a different place."

"But Mother. . ." Grace began to protest, amazed that she was even thinking of leaving Riverwood. What did it matter if she spent her life alone? What did anything matter if she hadn't Jonathan to love?

"We could take your mother with us, Grace."

Grace heard the words, weighed them in her mind, even turned slowly in his arms to look back at the house. Surely her mother would understand, would want her to be happy. Perhaps she could convince her mother to come along. . . .

But then she realized that Jonathan was turning her loose, and when she looked around she saw that he had put his hand over his forehead and was backing away from her.

"What am I saying?" he asked, then looked back at her as

though dazed. "Now I have really betrayed your father. Everything we've been doing is to carry out his mission for his farm and his family." He shook his head and began to walk quickly along the path to the barn.

Grace stared after him. She couldn't keep running after him; she couldn't keep begging. And he was right. If she turned Riverwood over to the bank, she would never forgive herself. Even if her mother would agree to go with them to Kentucky, Grace wouldn't feel right about it.

She turned slowly, feeling as though she had aged ten years in an hour. Her feet were leaden as she plodded back to the house, up the porch steps, and through the door. Like one in a trance, she put one foot in front of the other, climbing the stairs to her room. She closed the door, undressed, and went to bed. She didn't think she had the energy to ever get out of bed again. She rolled over on her stomach and covered her head with the pillow so she wouldn't hear General's hoofbeats as Jonathan left her. Forever.

thirteen

For two days Grace remained in bed. Her mother had wisely said little, bringing her trays of food that she later removed, the food cold and untouched. On the third day, Grace noticed that her mother wore a different look on her face.

"Grace, Isaac Banks is here. He wants me to tell you that he was laid off at the docks, once his foreman heard he was planning to leave. He's here to work. You have to get up now and tell him what you want done."

For a few minutes Grace lay unmoving, staring at the ceiling. Then slowly, she sat up and swung her legs over the side of the bed. The memory of Isaac's straightforward manner reminded her that she must treat him fairly; she had promised that. She got dressed and went downstairs.

Within a month, Isaac had rounded up enough men to clear the fields and burn off the old growth. He had done a splendid job of overseeing the men, and they worked from daylight to dark. Grace respected his position as overseer and only went to the fields to take food and water.

Grace had begun to join her mother on the porch each afternoon, for she felt lonely and sad, and it helped to have her mother to talk to. She was certain she would never feel really happy again, but she was at least beginning to have some satisfaction as she rode Lucky over the farm each day, inspecting the good job the men were doing.

One afternoon as she sat with her mother, she said, "Isaac

has accomplished so much. He tells me he'll have the land ready to plant in seeds by the first of the week. And after Mr. Britton came out to see for himself what is being done, he told me we can get another loan next year, if necessary."

Elizabeth patted Grace's hand. "You handled the situation well by paying off the loan but not stooping to say anything about his wife."

"I don't have the strength for another battle, Mother. I don't think anyone really wins a war. Not when you weigh the cost." She turned and looked at her mother. "You've taught me a lesson I'll never forget. You never wavered in your faith. You have remained a sweet loving person in spite of all the tragedy. When I compare you to others who are so bitter, I know the value of a close relationship with God."

Elizabeth nodded. "Even if everyone in the world thinks I'm foolish to keep sitting here waiting, hoping. . . ."

Grace shook her head and looked longingly down the driveway. "I would do the same if I thought I could see Jonathan riding up that drive again."

"Grace," her mother said, "can't you ask God for that and believe He will honor your faith?"

Grace looked at her mother and smiled. "I suppose I can."

The two women laughed together and sat back in their chairs, listening to the whippoorwill begin its evening song.

Grace was not sleepy that night and remained on the porch long after her mother had gone to bed. As she looked up at the vast sky overhead, amazed by all the stars and their special beauty, her mind moved on to the God who had created this beauty. She felt humbled and awed by such a God, and she stood up and walked over to the edge of the porch. Looking up in the night sky, a prayer began to form.

"Oh, God, please hear my prayer. I want to thank You for

sending Jonathan to us. I thank You for what my father did to try to protect and care for us. I thank You for the Bible he sent with his secret code. And I thank You for giving me the wisdom to understand that code.

"And then the gold, God. Thank You for the gold and for the difference it has made in our lives. But I have one more thing now that I must ask of You. Father, I love Jonathan, and I want to marry him and spend my life with him. I want us to have a family and to raise them in faith as my parents raised Freddy and me. I can better understand Your plan now, because of the way some things have happened. The way Father saved Jonathan, then Jonathan saved Father. Oh, God, I know that was in Your plan. And I do believe You want Jonathan and me to be together. Why else did You send him to us? Why *him?*

"I know that only You can touch our lives and work another miracle. Only You can heal the awful hate and anger between North and South; only You can patch up lives and hurts to where we can be together, either here or in Kentucky. I don't know how You could do this, God, but I know that You can. You are a mighty God."

She paused, taking a breath. She remembered the other prayers she had asked for—begged for, in fact—which God had not answered. He had not spared Freddy's life nor her father's life. And she had been angry and bitter.

"Father, I know I have offended You at times with all my fussing about life and the war and everything that has happened," she continued slowly. "But please, forgive me for the things I said and did. You promise in Your Word that if we confess our sins, You are faithful to forgive us. So please forgive me. And please bless Jonathan and me and let us have a future together. Please give us a chance for happiness." She took a deep breath. Hearing her words, she realized she didn't make much sense, but sometimes dreams didn't seem sensible. "Thank You for hearing this prayer and for helping us. And I'll try to be a better person. . ."

She kept her eyes closed for a few more minutes as the night silence settled over the porch, and a lonely little whippoorwill began to sing.

ʚ

That evening prayer brought Grace a sense of peace in the days to come. It was good to know she had asked God for forgiveness. Honoring the rest of that prayer was up to God, but she had ceased to fret over the outcome.

Sitting on the porch with her mother had become part of her daily routine. Grace even began to share her mother's pot of tea. She was still trying to build her faith, although it seemed that her mother had enough faith for both of them.

On Friday afternoon, after Isaac had paid the men and everyone had left for the weekend, Grace made sandwiches from fresh tomatoes out of the garden. They were eating vegetables for lunch every day now, and she was planning to go into Whites Creek to buy some chickens.

The two women had settled comfortably into their chairs after finishing their evening meal on the front porch and were listening for the whippoorwill. Grace could hear Lucky neighing from the pasture, and she smiled to herself, thinking how grateful she was to Jonathan for all he had helped her acquire. And to her father for providing the gold.

The whinny of a horse caught her ear, then she heard gravel crunching on the drive below.

"Who's coming on a Friday evening?" Grace wondered aloud.

Her mother looked at her with a twinkle in her eyes, but

Grace merely laughed and shook her head.

"Mother, it would be asking a lot for God to see Jonathan safely to Kentucky, get his business in order, then travel all the way back here in a month's time."

In spite of her words, Grace couldn't resist looking down the drive and feeling the tiny surge of hope that came to her each time a horse and rider drew near.

Two riders came around the curve and Grace sighed. "See, I told you. . ." Her voice trailed off into silence.

The first man rode a gray mare she had never seen, and he bent forward with a hat low on his forehead so that she couldn't make out who he was. But behind the first rider, she could see the side of a black horse. It was silly. She couldn't hope. She mustn't.

Her heart defied reason, however, for Grace leaned forward in her chair in an attempt to see around the lead horse and get a better look at the black horse.

Just then, the horses spread apart on the drive, and for a moment it seemed as though her heart had stopped beating.

Grace stood, her gaze fixed on the black horse. Then she saw the blazes on his legs and on his forehead. She ran down the steps, all the hope of her life centered in her heart as she watched the black horse come into clear view. At last she could see the rider.

A cry escaped her, and she stopped running, for tears blurred her vision, and her knees felt weak.

"Hello, Grace," Jonathan called to her. He swung down from the saddle and quickly covered the distance between them. They met in a wild embrace. He lifted her off her feet and swung her in the air.

She laughed and cried at the same time as she reached out to touch his face, feeling the stubble of beard beneath her fingertips. "I can't believe it," she said, wrapping her arms around him and hugging him tightly.

From behind her she heard her mother's voice. She knew her mother would be pleased to see Jonathan, but she couldn't share him, not yet.

"I've brought a visitor," Jonathan said.

But Grace wasn't paying attention. She tilted back her tear-stained face to look into Jonathan's eyes. Why didn't he kiss her? She couldn't wait much longer.

Then she heard her mother's voice again, this time an odd, strangled cry. Grace whirled around with concern. Her mother was running down the driveway toward the other horse. The man had swung down and was looking from her mother to Grace.

Grace reeled back against Jonathan. The world dipped and swayed. She couldn't believe her eyes. . .it couldn't be. But her mother's voice answered Grace's doubts. "Fred! I knew you would come back!"

Grace stood gaping in disbelief. The man was thin and stooped, but he was smiling and reaching out to her mother. As he turned and looked over his shoulder, Grace saw that he wasn't a dream. He was real. Her father had come home.

fourteen

It had taken an hour to settle everyone down, and in the end it had been Grace's mother who wisely suggested they go into the parlor where they would be more comfortable.

Grace hadn't left Jonathan's side; she never wanted to be separated from him again. She nestled against him on the love seat while her parents sat together, their chairs drawn close, their faces radiant with love.

"How?" Grace had asked the question a dozen times, unable to get beyond that single word.

Jonathan attempted to explain as they drank tea and left the food untouched. "After I left here that day, I couldn't forget the way your mother had waited so patiently for Mr. Cunningham; she had been so firm in her faith. And something she said to me on the porch that day continued to haunt me although I never said anything about it."

"What was it?" Elizabeth asked. Her face was radiant, her eyes glowing, and the love that softened her face gave her the appearance of a very young woman; she looked as though she were only a few years older than Grace.

"You asked me if your husband was alive when I left him. I had to admit that he was. I thought about that a lot, especially after I left here. I got to thinking, what if there is a chance he's still alive, just a chance? The more I pondered it, the more I knew I had to go back to the hospital to be sure. It was the only way I could get any peace for myself and for you."

He looked at Grace, and she saw that his eyes were filled with love for her. She wanted to cry with joy.

"When I got to the hospital, he was the first patient I saw. He was sitting out in the sun on a side porch, and I couldn't believe my eyes."

"I was going to be dismissed in a few days," Grace's father interjected, "but I hadn't wired you, Elizabeth, because the doctor had warned that we must be sure I was over the fever."

Grace listened intently as her father spoke. Her eyes drank in every feature of his face: the high arch of his brows, the wide-set gray eyes that seemed haggard and circled. Yet a light twinkled in the depths of those eyes and assured everyone that he was well.

"Jonathan told me everything that had happened." He looked from his wife to Grace, then he smiled at her. "He told me how strong and brave you have been, Grace. I am so proud of you."

"Father, I want to know how you ended up with that gold," she said. She had imagined a dozen different ways he could have acquired gold coins, and some of them were less than honorable. Yet she knew her father to be a honorable man.

"Another one of God's miracles," he said, leaning back in the chair.

Grace thought he was very thin, and he still looked terribly pale to her. Still, she knew if he had survived all that had happened to him, he would soon have all of his strength back, now that he was back at his beloved farm.

"It was the last week in September, and I was on a scouting patrol with another soldier. We were near Steven's Gap when we got ambushed by some Yanks. My buddy was killed, and my horse was killed, but I managed to hide in rocks and thick brush until morning. I climbed to the top of a mountain and looked down over the valley. I couldn't see any soldiers, so I figured they had moved on toward Chattanooga.

"In the valley, I spotted a bay horse grazing. Not seeing or hearing anyone, I crept toward the horse to investigate. As I got closer, I saw a Yankee soldier lying face down. I slipped up to him, after I was sure no one else was around. Being without a horse, my number one priority was to catch the bay. The horse kept feeding but would glance at me occasionally. Speaking gently, I walked toward the horse and noticed the nice saddle and brown leather saddlebags. The reins were still looped around the horse's neck, indicating the rider might have fallen from the saddle, possibly from illness or having been shot. Reaching the rein and tightly grasping it, I continued talking to the horse. I petted its neck with my left hand.

"My eyes were glued on the saddlebags, hoping they contained some ammunition and something to eat. I untied the leather straps of the saddlebag, lifted the flap, and looked in to see a leather bag with drawstrings pulled tight. When I picked the bag up and loosened its strings, I noticed how heavy it was. I looked inside and saw gold coins, a lot of them. Quickly I checked the offside bag. It too was full of coins. I hurriedly replaced the bags and retied them tightly. Then I searched the pockets of the dead soldier and found nothing but a small knife. He had no identification, nor any pistols or rifles.

"So I left him by the creek, mounted my new horse, rode to a thick, wooded area, and dismounted. Finding a clean spot on the ground, I emptied one bag and counted the money—six hundred dollars. The other bag had 720 dollars. That made a total of 1,320 dollars in gold coins."

Elizabeth reached out and touched her husband's hand. "Where do you think the money came from?"

"He wasn't an officer, and soldiers didn't carry that kind of money in their saddlebags. Because he was by himself and carrying money, I suspected it was stolen. I was alone, knowing that Yankee soldiers were in the area and more than likely between me and my outfit back on Lookout Mountain. So what should I do? If I hid the gold there and something happened to me, nobody would find it. I knew I had to find a safe place to hide the gold, a place where I could get a message to my family to go look for it. I sat praying for half an hour.

"Finally, I knew what I should do. A day's ride southwest would take me to the farm area where we lived before we moved to Pickens County. I figured if I could get on top of Sand Mountain, I wouldn't run into any Yanks. I asked God to see me safely there, and He did. I was led to the church and the apple tree. Even found the perfect smooth rock to carve my name on to use as a grave marker."

"And then you hid the money and rode back to your army?" Grace asked, completely amazed by what her father had told them.

"I did. And we don't need to talk about what happened after that. The best thing was that I met Jonathan here, and I realized he was a man I could trust. And I was right. Jonathan, I'll be indebted to you for the rest of my life."

"I'm just as indebted to you," he said, looking from Fred to Grace. "It was the only way I could have met your daughter, and I'll have to admit, Sir, that I haven't had a moment's peace since I left her."

"Nor have I," Grace said, smiling into his eyes.

"Fred, why don't we take your things upstairs? I'm sure

you need to rest after the long ride," Elizabeth suggested.

"How have you been?" Jonathan asked Grace after her parents had left the room.

Grace was vaguely aware that her parents had left them alone. She suspected they knew there were important things to be discussed, and this time Grace wasn't going to let Jonathan ride out of her life.

"I've been lonely. And sad. For all of my bragging about how much I loved this place, it didn't keep me from being lonely or from missing you with all my heart."

She reached forward and pressed her lips to his cheek. He took her in his arms. "Guess your mother will forgive me for breaking my promise, just this once," he said.

He drew her closer, and they kissed again and again. Finally he pulled away from her and stood. "Want to go with me to take care of the horses?"

She laughed. "Of course I do." As they walked out to the yard to lead the horses to the barn, she was already thinking how awful it would be when he started talking about leaving. She wanted to know how long he planned to stay, but she was too nervous to ask.

"Your father and I saw the fields and pastures. Everything looks nice, Grace."

"Isaac has been a miracle worker."

He reached out to pull her into his arms as they led the horses to the trough. "And I expect you've been quite the boss."

She laughed. "Actually, no. Isaac is his own man, you know. I didn't want to run the risk of losing him."

As they rubbed the horses down, Jonathan asked more questions about the farm, the cotton crop, even Reams and his wife.

She related everything to him, talking until she was almost hoarse. Then, as they walked back up to the house, she turned and looked at him.

"How long can you stay?" she asked, for she had to know.

"I sent another wire from Chattanooga," he said, looking serious. "This time I promised to be leaving here within the week."

"Oh." She nodded and looked down at the freshly cut grass beneath her feet. How could she say good-bye to him again? It would tear her heart out to spend time with him again, then watch him leave. She drew a deep breath. "I'll try hard not to beg you to stay," she said, but as she spoke, her throat tightened. She cast a glance toward her healthy garden, admiring row upon row of healthy vegetables that were her pride and delight.

Jonathan took her arm and turned her slowly to face him. "I believe we were standing about right here the last time I asked you to go home with me. You said you couldn't leave your mother alone. She's no longer alone," he said, trying to smile.

Grace searched his eyes, then turned and cast a glance toward the house. Her mind stumbled over his words, weighed them out, and as she did she wondered if she could really leave the only home she had ever known.

"I. . .don't know," she said, feeling his arms wrap around her. As she turned and looked into the deep blue eyes, she felt her heart start to beat in the way it always did whenever she was close to him. "I. . .Father just came home."

"Yes. That's why I planned to stay on a few days so you would have time to spend with him. Then, if you're willing, I thought maybe there could be a little service over in that church across the road."

"They're already having services—" She broke off as she

saw the twinkle in his eyes. "You mean like—?"

"Like a wedding," he said, tilting her chin back and smiling into her eyes. "Grace, if you'll marry me, I promise to do my best to be a good husband, a good father. I promise to be the kind of Christian man you deserve."

"You're already that kind of man, Jonathan," she said. "Do you really want to marry me?" she asked, suddenly feeling shy.

"As soon as I can. I don't know how much longer I can keep that promise to your mother."

They both laughed as they walked hand in hand back to the house. When they reached the kitchen, Grace's mother was busy preparing fresh vegetables.

"I can't wait to prepare a good meal for your father. And for you, Jonathan," Elizabeth said, smiling at him. "But first, Grace," she turned to look at her daughter, "your father wants to visit with you for a few minutes. He's resting in his bed."

"Of course." She looked at Jonathan.

"I'll stay here in the kitchen and see if your mother needs me to sample anything."

Grace laughed and left him settled at the table. She flew up the stairs to her parents' bedroom. Her father was not in bed, as she had expected. Instead he was seated in a rocking chair by the window. While her first impression of him had been that he was very thin and very tired, she knew when he turned his face to her and smiled that he was also very happy.

"Father, I'm so glad you're home." She ran to his side, throwing her arms around him and hugging him gently. She could feel his shoulder blades jutting out beneath his cotton shirt, but she knew between her mother and all the vegetables they had, he would soon be in good health again.

"Daughter, you can't possibly know how glad I am to be home." He turned and looked out the window.

Grace followed his gaze and saw that he was looking out on the cotton fields.

"You've done an amazing job, Grace. Jonathan has told me everything,"

"We have a wonderful overseer, Father. Isaac has accomplished miracles. Oh, I'm so glad you're here."

He looked at her, smiling affectionately. "There were times I wondered if I would ever see you and your mother again."

"She never stopped believing you would come home, Father. She never stopped looking and waiting for you. She always knew you would return. She has remarkable faith, and she has taught me a lot about waiting and trusting."

Grace paused, wondering how much Jonathan had told him about what they felt for each other.

"Pull up a chair," her father said, tilting his head back to study her thoughtfully. "You've turned into a beautiful woman, but then I always knew you would. And now I have something to ask you. How do you feel about Jonathan?"

Grace hesitated. She longed to tell him all that was in her heart, but she didn't want him to worry about her leaving. Now that she was sitting with him talking about Riverwood, she had begun to wonder if she could leave, even though she knew she was desperately in love.

"Speak up," he encouraged. "Are you half as smitten as he is? It's easy to see he is very much in love with you, Grace."

"And I'm that much in love with him, Father." She sighed, looking at her hands. "I just don't know what we can do about it."

"What do you mean?" He watched her closely, and she was certain she couldn't bear to hurt him. He had just come home to them; how could she tell him she wanted to leave?

"Well. . .he won't stay here, Father. I already asked him before."

"Of course not," her father readily agreed. "He has a farm in Kentucky, and he's long overdue to go see about it."

"But Father, he asked me to marry him," she blurted out. "He asked me to go back to Kentucky with him, and I can't do that." She was fighting not to cry, and she kept her head lowered so he wouldn't see the tears once they started rolling down her cheeks.

"Why can't you?" her father asked quietly.

For a moment Grace wasn't sure she had heard him correctly. Then slowly she lifted her head and looked into his eyes. When she did she saw the sheen of tears veiling his eyes.

She caught her breath. "Oh, Father, I won't leave you. Please don't be sad. I would never make you sad after what you've been through."

He shook his head and reached for her hand. "These are tears of joy. Grace, when I think of how blessed I have been to have a woman like Elizabeth, it chokes me up. I hate to think how empty my life would have been without her. As much as I love this farm, it would have meant nothing if I hadn't had Elizabeth as my wife, as the mother of our children. The joy and happiness of a good marriage is one of God's greatest gifts. Don't throw away that opportunity."

She stared at him, wondering if he understood that if she married Jonathan she would be leaving him and her mother.

"I would never want you to miss out on the happiness that your mother and I have known. Jonathan Parker is one of the finest men I have ever known. I would be proud to welcome him into our family."

"Father, I love him with all of my heart," she said, "but to marry him and move to Kentucky would be—"

"Would be what? Seems to me the man is planning a good life. He has talked to me a great deal about his ideas, and I can see that he's as crazy over horses as you've always been."

"Yes, he is." Grace laughed. "There's nothing I would rather do. But— Oh, Father, do you really think it would be all right for me to leave?"

He reached for her hand and held it against his chest. "Grace, no one could have been more brave or more conscientious than you have been in carrying on my work here. I'm not so selfish that I want to hang onto you for the rest of your life, though. And neither is your mother. We feel you deserve to be happy, and if you choose to find happiness with Jonathan, then you have our blessing."

"Oh, Father!" Grace leaned over to hug him as tears began to roll down her cheeks in spite of her efforts.

She knew she could wait no longer to tell Jonathan. All the sadness in her life had been magically wiped away, and she had been given an opportunity to live with Jonathan as his wife.

"Just be sure this is what you want," her father said, squeezing her hand.

She spoke slowly, confidently, for her words came straight from the heart. "I've never been more sure of anything in my life."

"Then I guess you and your mother had better get busy planning a wedding."

"I guess so." She laughed, then ran out of the room and down the stairs to the kitchen, wondering how to break the news to her mother. And what would Jonathan say when she told him she was going to accept his proposal?

Grace found them both in the kitchen, and her mother smiled at her, but there were tears in her eyes as well.

"You know?" Grace asked, looking at her mother carefully.

She nodded. "I've known all along."

Grace laughed and turned to Jonathan, who wrapped his arms around her. She thought she saw a light mist in his eyes as well.

He smiled and said, "The question is, do you know what *you* want to do?"

A lazy smile settled over her face. She took a deep breath and thought about their life together. "I know exactly what I want to do," she said, staring dreamily into his face. "I want to go to Kentucky as a bride, and I want to spend my life with you—and your horses," she added. They all broke into joyous laughter.

"Let's walk down to the garden," Jonathan suggested, glancing back at her mother. "I'm afraid if you start talking like that, it will be hard for me to keep my promise to your mother."

Grace laughed and nestled against his chest. "Soon you won't have to."

She could hear her mother's laughter following them down the hall as they went out on the front porch to gaze across the lawn. Twilight was settling over the land, and Grace could hear the whippoorwill starting its night song from the oak tree.

"I've waited here with Mother for what seems like an eternity," Grace said. "I've waited for you, Jonathan. I prayed for you to come back to me. And now you have." She shook her head in amazement. She still couldn't believe all that had happened.

"Yes, now I have," he said, wrapping her in his arms again.

"And I never want to leave you again."

She smiled as he lowered his lips to hers. "I won't let you leave me."

She knew she sounded a bit sassy, but she could feel her teasing spirit surging forth again. She felt something else, though, something much stronger. She felt the deep abiding love that she knew her parents shared. With that knowledge, like her mother, she would always be waiting for Jonathan to ride home each evening, to take her in his arms, and to share the rest of their lives together.

A Letter To Our Readers

Dear Reader:

In order that we might better contribute to your reading enjoyment, we would appreciate your taking a few minutes to respond to the following questions. We welcome your comments and read each form and letter we receive. When completed, please return to the following:

Rebecca Germany, Fiction Editor
Heartsong Presents
PO Box 719
Uhrichsville, Ohio 44683

1. Did you enjoy reading *My Beloved Waits* by Peggy Darty?
   ❏ Very much! I would like to see more books by this author!
   ❏ Moderately. I would have enjoyed it more if

   _____

   _____

   _____

2. Are you a member of **Heartsong Presents**? Yes ❏ No ❏
   If no, where did you purchase this book?_____

   _____

3. How would you rate, on a scale from 1 (poor) to 5 (superior), the cover design?_____

4. On a scale from 1 (poor) to 10 (superior), please rate the following elements.

   _____ Heroine   _____ Plot

   _____ Hero   _____ Inspirational theme

   _____ Setting   _____ Secondary characters

5. These characters were special because_____

_____

_____

6. How has this book inspired your life?_____

_____

_____

7. What settings would you like to see covered in future
   Heartsong Presents books?_____

_____

_____

8. What are some inspirational themes you would like to see
   treated in future books?_____

_____

_____

9. Would you be interested in reading other **Heartsong
   Presents** titles?   Yes ❑   No ❑

10. Please check your age range:
    ❑ Under 18   ❑ 18-24   ❑ 25-34
    ❑ 35-45   ❑ 46-55   ❑ Over 55

Name _____

Occupation _____

Address _____

City _____ State _____ Zip _____

Email _____

KANSAS

*S*urviving the harsh prairie elements—like surviving the storms of the heart—takes faith and determination, which four young women need to prove they possess. Can their hearts hold fast against the gales that buffet them? Will they find love waiting at the end of the storm?

Love on the Kansas prairie is hard and unpredictable. . .but also as inevitable as an early summer cyclone. Watch in wonder as God turns the storms of life into seasons of growth and joy.

paperback, 464 pages, 5 ¾₁₆" x 8"